SLAMMING THE ORC

MONSTER ORCS OF PROTHEKA
BOOK THREE

MILLY TAIDEN

CELESTE KING

SLAMMING THE ORC

MONSTER ORCS OF PROTHEKA

NEW YORK TIMES AND USA TODAY
BESTSELLING AUTHOR
MILLY TAIDEN

&

CELESTE KING

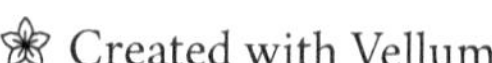 Created with Vellum

ABOUT THE BOOK

It's survival of the fittest.

My sister and I are not the fittest. Hell.

Still, we've survived.

But dark elves and orcs control earth.

Only, now we're surrounded.

We need a knight in shining armor to save us.

Well, how about in a shining loincloth instead?

I am Jovak,

Orc chieftain of the Shattered Rock tribe.

I've just interrupted some orcs trying to eat humans.

But when I see Paige, I know I need to save her.

She's the one. My one.

My problems are bigger than even I know.

My tribe is in trouble.

There are those trying to take my power.

Several of my people have gone missing.

Strange magic and the beautiful Paige are the solutions to my problems.

I just need to convince her that she's stronger that she realizes.

So strong she's the only one I need.

—I hope you're enjoying the world of the Orcs of Protheka. Get ready for a wild ride!

PAIGE

Acrid smoke stings my nostrils as I move up the steep hill in a slow crawl. There's no sound but that of ravens cawing with delight over their huge feast. Honestly, I'm not sure what the orcs and dark elves are accomplishing with their turf wars other than feeding the birds. They are all going to be some fat fuckers after all this.

A battlefield between two immensely powerful races of beings is probably the last place a human woman like me should be. Especially considering I've brought along my ten-year-old sister, who's currently hiding in a copse of trees at the bottom of this hill.

Make that she's supposed to be hiding. I can see

her little face peeking out from behind a tuft of waist-high grass. She ducked down among the bent and drooping blades when she sees me looking back, but she's a second too late.

I grimaced, but there's not much I can do about it. Not until I know what's waiting for us on the other side of the hill. We saw the lights and heard the clash of the armies when we were hiking through this area yesterday.

It seems like the battle is done, but that doesn't mean it really is. I have to look over the hill and make sure we're actually alone. If there is even one solitary dark elf or orc, we'll turn back and forget it.

If, however, the coast happens to be clear, we can scavenge the battlefield. There's a surprising number of useful items left behind when two armies clash, and if you're clever and patient, you can pick them up for yourself.

Of course, you have to deal with the smell of burnt flesh and the occasional rotting body, but this is a harsh world, and you do what you must to survive.

I reached the top of the hill, my hands gripping a half-buried limestone rock for support. I pulled myself up enough to peer over to the other side. I'm expecting carnage, and I am not disappointed.

The battle was fought in a valley that was probably pleasant beforehand. An orcish war machine lies on its side, all but one wheel busted off and half-burned into a charred, black mockery of its former function. Several fires are still burning here and there, one of them a pile of corpses. I make a mental note to stay upwind of that particular gore. The dark elves take their warriors' bodies back while the orcs mainly burn them on the battlefield, taking only the sometimes-broken weapons back to be given to the next generation.

And as for humans, we usually burn our dead because nobody has the time or patience for burial any longer.

I glance over my shoulder and see Laney peeping out from behind the bush again. I motion for her to come up and join me as I stand up. Laney makes it up the hill even faster than me, her spindly limbs moving like cyclones.

"Wow," she says when she stands beside me. "You weren't kidding when you said it was a big battle. I wonder who won."

"It's hard to tell. Come on, let's get what we need and get out of here before any more scavengers come along." I sigh. What is the use of fighting every battle with Laney?

"You have a sword. I have my knife," she says, brandishing a knife so tiny it could only be dangerous to a rabbit. "Let them try to take our stuff."

I grimace at my sister, putting my hands on my hips. I hate how this war has made Laney grow up so fast. I sometimes don't even recognize her anymore.

"I have a sword, yes, but I hope I never have to use it. You should hope that too. Don't go looking for trouble, sis. You'll always find it."

"You sound like Grandpa."

"Grandpa was smart. And so are you when you remember to stop acting like some epic hero in a story."

The wind shifts, and the plumes of smoke drift our way. The smoke obscures the hillside we stand on like the fog of war. I start down the slope before I get a good whiff of the pile of burning corpses.

Laney follows along behind. Her prattle diminishes the farther we get down into the valley. At the bottom, she goes into a grim silence. She may be scrappy, but standing knee-deep among the dead is going to put a damper on anyone's spirits.

We carefully pick our way through broken swords, sundered spears, and bits of metal armor, most stained with blood. The flies are going crazy on some of the bodies. One orc corpse has so many flies covering it that it appears as black as midnight.

I come upon a wagon upthrust from the ground. A pile of dirt and jagged rock protrudes from the covered top, making the whole thing sit askew.

"What happened here?" Laney asks, her voice unnaturally loud in the deathly quiet.

"Shh," I say, holding my finger to my lips. I respond in a soft, quiet tone. "It looks like dark elf sorcery to me. They can make the ground come up like that under their enemies."

"Cool."

"No, not cool. Not if you're on the receiving end." I intertwine my fingers and squat to give Lancy a foothold to step into. "I'll give you a boost up. See if there's anything worth salvaging in there."

She puts her foot in my stirrup hands, and I lift her until she disappears over the edge. I hear her thumping around.

"It's pretty dark, but I think I can rip a hole in the canopy to let in more sunlight."

A ripping sound, then Laney gasps.

"There's a bunch of salted jerky in here."

"Salted jerky?" My belly grumbles. We've had nothing to eat for days but roots and berries. Protein sounds like the cure for my trembling limbs. "Start tossing it down."

We stack the jerky and some hardtack bread too. The bread is not appetizing in the least and requires half a waterskin to wash down a mouthful, but it's sustenance, and I can't bear to leave it behind.

"Okay, that's enough." I put my hands on my hips and stare at the collection we've amassed. "That's all we can carry up the hill at once. I think we should load it on the wagon and get on the road north."

"Why north?"

"Because the army that won this battle headed south, judging by the tracks."

We carry our burdens up the hill and down the other side. I'm glazed with sweat by the time we make it to the bottom. Our wagon has seen better days, but it still functions. Ditto for the old onager that pulls it. The donkey brays and flicks its ears in worry.

"What's wrong, girl?" I ask, putting my hand on her neck.

"Maybe she doesn't like thieves."

I turn around quickly, one hand falling to the hilt of the curved sword I don't even know how to use. A group of six orcs stands nearby, all of them wearing black leather with splashes of crimson. I know the symbol on their armor, a wavy red line with a fanged mouth. The Red Wyrm Clan.

Not one of the orc clans that live peaceably with humans, not by a long shot. I wouldn't be so worried if it were the Crimson Sun Clan.

"Laney," I whispered so only she could hear me. "I want you to run. Now. As far and as fast as you can."

"But I want to help ..."

"Remember what Grampa said?" I snap. "I'm in charge. Now run! I'll find you later."

Laney gives me a withering look, then turns and bolts up the hill toward the battlefield.

"Neska, go get the little one," one of the orcs says. "She's just about the right size for the stewpot."

"You won't touch her!"

I manage to draw the sword without looking like a total novice, but as soon as I hold the awkward weight in my hand, I feel more afraid, not less. The lead orc laughs and looks at his band with a big grin on his face.

"Oh no, whatever will we do? I guess we'd better surrender before this fierce warrior slays us all." His sarcasm is enough to make the other orcs laugh.

"We just want to be left alone," I say, my voice trembling and my knees shaking badly. The lead orc casually walks toward me, his weapon still at his side.

"Now, come on," he says. "All you're going to do is make things harder on yourself."

He holds out his hand, palm up.

"Give me the sword."

Poor choice of words.

I swing the sword down with all my might. The orc leader withdraws his hand, but not quickly enough. He screams as two of his fingers fall almost noiselessly to the grass, rapidly staining the green to red with his blood.

I try to finish him off, but two more orcs are on me before I can take a full breath. One of them batters the sword right out of my hand, leaving my whole arm numb. The other grabs my shirt collar and throws me into the trunk of a tree.

I fly backward, and then everything gets hazy for a bit. I think I passed out a couple of times, but I keep forcing myself awake because of Laney. By the time I'm cognizant enough to put two thoughts together, I'm staring out the iron bars of a cage, and Laney is sitting beside me.

I gasp and touch the side of her head. There's a red welt there. The orcs knocked her out brutally. I guess if they want to eat her, they don't care if they scramble her brains.

I fear the orcs are going to do even worse with me than they will with her. I reach into the secret pocket sewn into my pantaloons. The knife is still there. They didn't even bother to search me.

I draw the knife, not to use on the orcs, but to use on Laney and then myself. It's the only way I can spare her the suffering that's sure to come.

"I'm sorry, Laney," I whisper under my breath as the orcs fuss about with our wagon. They remove everything of value, including the onager, and then set it on fire with a lot of whooping and hollering.

I worked hard to find and repair that wagon.

It's taken us thousands of miles, and now it's going to burn to ash.

It's not fair. Nothing has been fair for us humans since the orcs and dark elves invaded. All we can do is try to mitigate our suffering.

Like I'm going to do now. This is what I promised my grandad on his deathbed. That if the time came, I would not allow myself and Laney to be captured. I would set us free in a way that could not be undone.

I hold the knife to my sister's snow-white throat. My vision blurs with tears. I can't bring myself to do it. I can't.

I stuff the knife back in the secret pocket and hold my sister tight. Tears stream down my face. The orcs think it's hilarious. My pain and misery are entertainment for their lot.

I don't even care anymore. Nothing matters. I can't bring myself to fulfill my vow because I can't bear to kill my little sister. I could probably turn the blade on myself with less effort. There's no way I can take the easy way out and leave my little sister to suffer.

What are we going to do?

2

JOVAK

Red sun, red water.

Normally that only happens when the rising sun hits this old pond just right. But not today. The red sun is setting, not rising. The angle is all wrong.

Still, it's not hard to tell what turned the waters crimson. The pile of dead orcs lay sprawled across the rocky shore of the pond, their bodies twisted and mangled. Even though they're the brutal and untrustworthy Red Wyrm Clan, I still mourn for them. They are orcs, after all. My people who were slaughtered by dark elves.

It looks like their little company was separated from the main battle unit and then forced to retreat until they wound up at the pond. Then the elves slaughtered them. Several green-gray bodies float in the water, so many arrows sticking out of them they look like hedgehogs. No doubt the dark elves continued their sport even after the swimming orcs were long dead.

I wonder how many others of my brethren lie beneath those murky waters. As I said, there is nothing I can do for them. It is all I can do to keep my own Shattered Rock tribe safe.

That's the only reason I've ranged so far from our territory. Usually, my walks don't take me away for more than a day or two. But once I saw the dark elf army on the march, I had to follow in order to assess the danger to my own tribe.

Of course, after three days of following in their wake, it became apparent they were not going anywhere near my tribe's land. After that point, I was just indulging my penchant for wandering.

Being the chief is a heavy burden to bear. I have to get away sometimes. I'm just not normally gone this long. I can already imagine what they're saying about me. How I've shirked my responsibilities as their leader again.

Still, I've gone too far now to stop. I need to see this through just in case the dark elves are a threat to my tribe. Yesterday one of the rear guards of the dark elf army spotted me, and I had to flee for many hours to escape him.

Thus, I'm at least a day and a half too late to witness the battle. Judging from the smoke trailing into the red-gold skies, I'd say that it was quite the blaze. I can smell the burned bodies and the start of rot already.

The acrid smell of fresh smoke stings my nostrils. My eyes narrow, and I reach to my belt for the twin axes I keep there. Perhaps this battle is not completely over after all.

If I see a chance to bury my blades in the skulls of some dark elves, I'll gladly take it. And if the Red Wyrm tribe wants to tangle with me, they'll get the same. I am the greatest warrior of my tribe … a tribe made up of exceptionally great warriors.

We've held the shattered rock far longer than most of the other clans have existed. All creatures, great and small, fear our arrows, our spears, and our blades.

My great-great-grandfather came through the portals from Protheka, fleeing the dark elves and their damnable ways. Here, we found a new species that called themselves human beings. Their technology didn't save them from us in the early days when magic still coursed through our veins like liquid fire.

We no longer hunt and oppress the humans. The Chief of the Crimson Sun has taught us a better way. The humans might be weaker than us, smaller … but they are very crafty, industrious, and more capable in battle than their size would suggest.

Some of my tribe members have even taken humans as their mates. I am not one of them. When I mate, it must be with an orc female. Since there are few fertile orc females being born any longer, I have been mateless for the entirety of the ten years I have led the tribe.

The truth is I'm content with this. If I had a mate, she would no doubt object to my spending long periods of time away from home. I would not be able to wander. They would no longer call me Jovak the Longstrider. What would they call me, Jovak the Tamed? Jovak the Housebroken?

The axes feel good in my hands. Their weight is a comfort to me. In these axes, I can put my trust. One of them is ancient, wrought with numerous runes and embossed ivy leaves on the black metal blade. A minor enchantment that hasn't entirely faded makes the blade immune to corrosion or rust. The handle has been replaced several times, but otherwise, it is still the same ax my …

I shake my head. No, no good bringing up that memory. I endure the shame of it enough as it is. I have no room in my head for cloudiness. I must keep my mind, body, and spirit ready for whatever awaits me on the other side of this hill.

My second ax is of human manufacture. The entire thing, from hilt to angled cutting edge, is made of metal, and a damn fine steel it is too. The red paint has long worn off the handle, as well as the business end, but some traces of it remain near the pommel and the conjunction between handle and blade.

I found this ax inside of a crumbling human structure. It was within a glass case hanging on a wall as if it were to be protected or perhaps revered. I took it because it looked sturdy enough to use as a tool or a weapon, but I mainly use it to cut flesh, not wood.

I was told by one of the humans at our camp that this ax belonged to a special class of humans called *firefighters*. Of course, I'm not sure how much good an ax would be against a fire. It seems like a bucket, and a source of water would be far more useful.

I had hoped that my people would start calling me Jovak Two-Edge rather than Longstrider, but it didn't take. My tendency to wander alone has been ingrained deeply in how my tribe sees me.

Whatever is waiting for me over that hill could be hostile. Or there could be nothing, just more dead bodies torn asunder by steel or spell.

I lean in and let my long, powerful legs eat up the terrain. All of the walking I do has made me leaner than most of my kin. That, and … but it's not important right now. All that's important is keeping myself on the edge of readiness in case I have to do battle.

The top of the hill approaches. I stand straighter and find myself atop a steep incline leading down into a little valley. It was probably a pleasant valley for a walk at one time before the battle. Now the green grass is torn and burned, charred black. Trees lay sundered into a thousand splinters by magically produced lightning bolts. And, of course, the dead are everywhere. I believe the dark elves won because I don't see any of their bodies laying about. They must have collected their dead.

But not all of the Red Wyrm tribe have departed. I see a half dozen milling about at the base of the hill. And they see me. One of them looks up, his helm flashing in the dying rays of the setting sun. He points at me, and the others look my way.

Damnation, I hadn't wanted them to spot me. Now, I have to make a decision. They would have to fight their way up this steep hill to reach me, in which case I could easily run back down the other side and disappear into the woods before they could find me.

Or I could charge down this hill and slay them all. My blood burns for battle. I am an orc, after all. Or, at least, mostly.

But it would be irresponsible for me to indulge in my bloodlust when my tribe has not heard from me in days. I should probably leave. They don't seem overly interested in trying to come after me, anyway.

I see why a moment later. They have prisoners. Two forms huddle together inside an iron cage on the back of an orcish wagon. Dark elves? No, not likely. They are too small. Humans are my best guess. Humans who came to scavenge among the dead a bit too soon, or perhaps, too late.

Not my concern, of course. So what will it be, Jovak? Will you charge down there and seek battle among the Red Wyrm Clan? Or will you turn and flee to your own people and toward the responsibilities you have shirked for far too long?

Then, I hear something that decides the matter for me.

I hear a child scream.

3

PAIGE

A few moments ago, I was locked in a cage awaiting an uncertain fate. Now I'm outside, ostensibly free, and my fate is certain.

That doesn't mean my fate is going to be any more or less pleasant, however.

It all happened so fast. I'd been holding Laney against me as she recovered. The orcs milled around, watching my wagon burn while one of their scouts picked over the rest of the battlefield just to be certain they hadn't missed anything of value.

The orcs had all looked up the hill Laney and I had descended not so long before this. I couldn't make out what they were so upset about because the cage's wooden roof blocked my vision. I figured it was trouble, though, from the way they all gripped the hilts of their weapons.

One of the orcs said something I couldn't make out ... I think it was the orc word for *enemy* ... and then they began making their way up the hill. All save one.

The smallest, weakest orc of them all remained behind. His green eyes locked with my gaze, and I knew what he had on his mind. Revolting as it was, I was more worried about Laney's fate than my own.

"Come here, you," he said, throwing the cage door open. "You're mine. Sleesak will no longer have to wait for the bruised, battered, and whimpering seconds."

His hand closed on my wrist, and he dragged me out of the cage. Even though he was small for an orc, he was still many times stronger than me.

Laney had recovered at that point and tried to stop him, throwing a rock that dinged off the orc's helmet. He almost casually backhanded Laney, sending her tumbling to the ground. Laney's scream of rage and despair could have been mistaken for fear by someone who didn't know her as well as I did.

Seeing my kid sister smacked down like a common dog made my blood boil. I grabbed the nearest weapon I could find, an orc sword. The damn thing was *heavy*, but I got it up in front of me with two hands on the hilt. I stood between the orc and Laney.

This brings me to the present. The other orcs are shouting and causing a ruckus on the hill, but I don't dare take my eyes off what's going on right in front of me.

"Oh, look at her," he says with a snicker. "You won't be cutting *my* fingers off, little meat."

"I was thinking of something a little lower," I snarl. "Something you'll be sure to miss."

He tilts his head back and laughs at me. It burns my pride, which is stupid, considering I should be way more worried about my hide. Hide, not pride.

"Laney," I cry. "Run! Get out of here."

I spare a glance for Laney, and my heart sinks to my feet. She's been stunned by the orc's blow, groggy and bleeding in the dirt.

"Yes, Laney," the orc sneers. "Run! Get up and run so you won't have to see what I do to your big sister."

I glance at Laney again and then at the orc. I let the sword droop in my grip a bit. Actually, I don't know how much of it is me letting it droop and how much is because my arms just can't hold it up any longer. I would have to snatch up one of the bigger orc swords. Too late to do anything about it now.

"Listen," I say, my voice breaking as my lips suddenly go dry, "if you let my sister go, you can have me."

"I can have you in any case," he growls.

I hear the clash of steel from up on the hill. His eyes dart that way and then back to me.

"You'll have to force me, and you don't have time for that." My eyes narrow. "You don't want bruised, whimpering seconds, do you?"

His face contorts into a mask of contempt and rage. The worst thing you can do is point out a man's inadequacies to him, even if he's an orc. *Especially* if he's an orc.

"If you'll let my sister go," I say, my voice steadier this time. "I won't fight you. I'll … I'll make it good."

My face burns with shame. Like I would know how to make it good. When it comes to fleshly pleasures, I haven't had the pleasure, so to speak. I'd listened to the older girls growing up, though, and I know a little bit about the carnal act.

Enough to know that it's a lot better when you cooperate.

Then again, some orcs like it when women fight back.

"Oh, you'll make it good," he snarls. "You don't get to drive bargains with me."

He takes a step toward me, and I lift the sword point between us. I guess an adrenaline surge is going through me because the sword barely wavers now.

"Then I'll sell myself as dearly as I can." My voice sounds so fierce I almost believe myself. "Maybe I can't win against you, but I can hurt you. I can make you suffer."

"Weak lower form," he snarls. "You're the only one who is going to suffer."

"Try me." I wish I was half as confident as I sound. I don't have to win this fight. I just have to stall this orc long enough that Laney can recover and escape.

"Oh, I will."

"Then do it," I snap.

He licks his thick lips, and his eyes grow narrow and crafty. He's not advancing on me. Obviously, he doesn't know how much of a novice I am with a sword. Or how hard it is just to hold the stupid thing up, let alone swing it. Otherwise, he'd have overrun me by now.

Then again, I remember my grandpa talking about everyone having a *puncher's chance* in a fight. Even a weak or unskilled opponent could hurt you if you didn't take them seriously enough.

I decide to play on his fears and force a cavalier smile on my face.

"Come on, Sleesak," I snarl. "You won't be the first orc to split himself on my blade. Maybe I'll take your armor and your balls as a souvenir."

He growls. It is a low and primal sound like an animal might make. I've done it now. I've made him angry. If I were a master swordsman or even just one with training, I might be able to take advantage of his rage. Lure him into making a mistake. Alas, as it stands, I don't have that option.

Apparently, the orc has more caution than anger in him. He grins and lets his own sword droop down.

"Come, now," he says in what he probably considers a reasonable tone. "There's no point in making this hard on yourself or your sister. If you'll put down the sword and be a good girl, I'll tell the others she's too mangy and diseased for the stew pot."

"No chance. You want me to put this sword down. You let her go first."

Laney struggles to her feet, then flops back down to her bottom. Her brains seem scrambled. I hope she doesn't have a skull fracture. That can be lethal without a doctor, and there are not many of those left. I guess a shaman might be able to help, but I don't see one of those around either.

She needs help. She can't run. I have to find a way to win this fight, somehow.

"I don't think she's going anywhere," he says with a sick grin.

Yeah, I don't think she is, either. I have to win … I have to *win*. But how? How do I defeat a far more experienced opponent who can throw me around like a rag doll? My wrist still hurts from where he grabbed it earlier.

I need to trick him. Make him think I'm helpless, maybe.

He tries to circle around to where he can reach Laney, but I move in sync with him, keeping his path blocked. But as I move, I let myself stumble a bit. My movements are awkward and clumsy. On purpose, I mean. I should probably say, more awkward and clumsy than usual.

"Don't let it cross your mind that I mind raping

a dead girl," he growls. "Or one with all of her limbs removed. We can burn the wounds shut, so you don't bleed out and keep you around for days. All of the important parts will be left, or at least the three holes I care about."

Ignoring his revolting commentary, I let the sword point dip a bit and grunt as if it's taking effort to keep it up. Hell, it *is* taking effort, but I feign that it's a lot worse than it actually is.

"You can't even hold that sword, let alone swing it."

"Fuck you," I sputter as if I'm losing control. He grins and stops circling. Sleesak stands to his full height ... dropping his guard in the process, but I can't land a hit before he raises it again ... and taps the flat of his blade onto his thick, meaty palm.

"All I have to do is wait until you can't hold that blade any longer. Ah, there it goes now."

"No," I scream in defiance. I'm so terrified and upset I hardly have to pretend. "No!"

I let the sword shake badly in my grip, and then with a groan of despair, the tip drops to the dirt.

"There we go," he snarls, racing toward me. He lifts his sword over his head for a two-handed blow, a killing blow. I guess he's more interested in sating his anger than other baser desires.

Just as he steps in, I lift the tip right at his belly. He puts on the brakes, but it's too late. Sleesak runs right into my sword.

The impact nearly wrenches the blade from my grasp. He gasps, his mouth flying open in a wide O. He staggers back, fingers pressed against the blood seeping from between them to run down his front.

"You cut me," he says in horror and indignation. "You cut my flesh!"

"Yeah, well, I was hoping to kill you," I say. I move in and try to finish him off, but his sword arm hasn't slowed one iota. He bats my attack aside and swings at me, sending my sword spinning end over end through the air to clatter uselessly to the ground.

"Now you and your sister will die screaming," the orc growls. My blow isn't lethal. It barely even slows him down.

I silently apologize to Laney as death creeps toward me.

4

JOVAK

My duty is to my tribe. But there is no way I could live with myself if I'd let the Red Wyrm tribe do the unspeakable to a child. Even if that child is merely human.

I cross the crest of the hill and then plunge down the other side in a dead run. My legs move in a blur as I struggle to keep the run from turning into an uncontrolled tumble. My first foe is a bit too eager. He hauls himself up the slope, leading with his spear point. No doubt, he thinks that his greater reach will skewer me before I can bring my dual axes to bear.

Only I am prepared for just such a maneuver. When we're just a few paces away, he makes his move, taking the haft of his spear in two hands and thrusting it upward. My black ax chops down hard on the spearpoint, chipping a fingertip-sized chunk out of the blade.

My red ax leaves his skull in pieces. Unfortunately, it gets stuck, and I leave it impaled in his head and leap over his falling body. I raise my remaining weapon in a two-handed grip and drop nearly fifteen feet before I swing it at the next Wyrm.

He raises his shield to parry the blow. I smash him to the ground, my blade deflecting off his shield ... but while the metal of his shield protected him from my cutting edge, it didn't hinder the impact a bit. The satisfying crunch of broken bone reaches my ears as his shield arm shatters.

He tumbles violently down the hill, but I have no time to worry about this foe. My next is already preparing to meet me. Having seen the fate of his brethren, this one is moving with more caution.

I can't help but notice this orc is already wounded. His right hand is missing some fingers, and the bandage wrapped around the stumps is soaked with blood. A recent injury then, not one from the great battle. That's good for me. Pain can make a warrior more alert, but it can also hinder his ability to think on his feet.

Unfortunately for me, he's not alone. Another orc joins him, and from the way they adjust their stances, I can tell they're used to fighting together. I slow my charge and come to a halt, blinking sweat out of my eyes. Never taking my sight off my enemies for even a second, I crouch and pluck a short sword from the battlefield. The tip is shorn off, leaving behind a jagged bit, but it should still be plenty lethal.

"Now is the time to run," snarls the one missing fingers. I think he might be the leader, judging by the tattoos on his flesh.

"Yes, it is," I reply. "I'm in a generous mood. I might not chase you down and slay you if you're quick about it."

The leader growls, his eyes narrowing to dangerous yellow slits. The other orc sneers as if he thinks I'm full of bravado, but not much sense.

I spare a glance at the caged humans … and find they're no longer in the cage. I don't see what happened to the little one, the child … I hope I'm not too late … but the other one, the adult, faces off against the remaining Wyrm.

Brave of her to go against a clearly superior foe,

especially with a sword she can barely control. I'm impressed, indeed, but I can't help her. Not with these two in my way.

I try a feint with the broken sword, but they see it coming and don't take the bait. They attack in unison, and I parry both of their weapons with my sword and ax.

They try to bowl me over with raw strength. I hold them at bay. Even when they put so much effort into it, their bodies tremble.

"Take him down," snarls the leader through gritted teeth.

"I'm trying," the other snarls. "He's too … strong."

Strong and smart. I pivot on my back leg and turn my body to the side. The two orcs get in each other's way, and I manage to take a chunk out of the leader's shoulder with my ax.

He howls and staggers back, clapping his wounded shoulder with his equally wounded hand. His fellow narrows his gaze and then grins at me.

"I should thank you. No doubt I will be named the new leader of our war band, given that you've crippled him."

"Damn your tongue, Drietak," snaps the leader. "I'm hardly crippled."

Out of pride or maybe fear of losing his position, the leader comes in again, ignoring the blood pouring out of the hole in his shoulder. They might be Red Wyrms, but they are orcs. They will continue to fight until they can't.

I hear a hard blow from the vicinity of the human woman. I still haven't gotten a look at her face, but I think she's on the young side, though still an adult. I spare a glance her way and see the woman holding her wrist, her sword flopping to the ground a dozen feet away.

The orc she'd been battling sneers and moves in for the death blow. I've no more time to deal with these two. In another moment, the woman will be skewered.

When I was first learning to use weapons, the man at arms told me that there was one cardinal rule of combat. You never, ever, ever let go of your weapon on purpose. Even if you had a spear, you didn't throw it. That was reserved for javelins.

Yet, that's exactly what I do. I send the red ax spinning end over end through the air. The leader tries to get his sword up in time to block, but the chaotic flight path of the ax throws him off. The edge buries itself in his face. The leader's eyes go wide as if in shock. He falls forward to his knees, then collapses but doesn't land on his belly. The haft of the ax imbeds in the ground, leaving his body grotesquely propped up in an ungainly position.

His fellow orc apparently isn't as concerned with a promotion as he indicated. He throws himself at me with a rage reserved for mated pairs. I parry his powerful but clumsy strikes, the whole time worried that the woman was already dead.

Then he overextends his thrust, an error he won't live to regret. While his blade is out and no longer protecting his body, I shove the broken end of the sword right through his heart.

I yank the blade back out, not even bothering to check to see if he's dead. He's at least incapacitated for the time being.

I turn toward the last orc, who holds his sword high in the air. The woman stands protectively over the child, holding her arms up as a feeble shield against the blade that is about to spell doom for them both.

I have no time. I throw the short sword, but it's not as balanced as my ax. It flies crazily off to the side, missing the orc by a few feet. However, it does get his attention, which buys the woman another precious second or two.

He turns toward me just as I reach him. I drop my shoulder to the level of his breadbasket and lunge forward, striking him in the solar plexus. The air whooshes out of his lungs in a ragged gasp, and we both go down. He still has a grip on his sword, but at this close range, it's not going to do him any good.

There is no grace, no nobility, and no mercy in orc grappling arts. I sink my teeth into his ear and rip off a chunk while he scratches his nails down my face, slashing my eyelid. I hiss, blood flowing into my eye and blinding me on that side. We roll around in the dirt, and he finally gives up the sword. We each seek the advantage, struggling for dominance. I slam my knee into his crotch and wind up straddling him on the blood-soaked ground.

I lift my hands and bring them down in a double-fisted blow across his face. His nose smashes flat, shards of bone shooting out through the skin. I repeat the blow again and again, using his head like a drum until he stops twitching. His chest rises and falls, rises and falls … and then lies still.

I get off the orc and check the others. All dead, save the one with the broken arm, and all he can do is lie on the ground and moan.

I turn to the woman, who scrambles back in the dirt, her eyes wide with fear. My breath catches in my throat. I have seldom seen such a lovely example of a human woman. I never thought I would like a woman without at least a wart or two, but her freckled skin and heart-shaped face have their own appeal.

She has a lovely form, but she's terrified, and for some reason, that bothers me. I don't want her to fear me.

"I'm not going to hurt you," I say, holding my hands up. "I'm not even armed."

"Armed?" she looks at the carnage I have wrought. "You don't need a weapon; you *are* a fucking weapon."

I chuckle softly and shrug.

"Perhaps that is true. However, this weapon is not meant to harm you." I gesture at the groaning child. "How fares the youngling?"

She seems to remember the child about then. Still keeping a wary eye on me, she crawls to the girl and then gently shakes her.

"Laney," she says. "Are you all right?"

The child mutters something and tries to open her eyes. I see a large knot swelling on the side of her head. My anger boils over. Only the lowest of the low would harm a child, no matter what species they are from.

I reach into my belt pouch and pull out some somerset seeds. Then I crouch beside the two humans. The older one startles, but then she sees the seeds in my hand.

I chew them into a paste, then spit it into my palm. I know she doesn't want me to touch the child, so I offer her the remedy.

"Here," I say. "Put it in the wound. It will help."

She reaches for the paste, not upset that it's been in my mouth. She keeps giving me looks, though, like she thinks I could go crazy and harm her or the child at any moment.

I provide a strip of leather to use as a bandage, again being careful not to get too close to the child. I think the child might be her daughter. They have similar sandy-blonde hair and freckles.

"Thank you," she says. Then we stare at each other. She's waiting for me to say or do something, but what?

I need to get back to my tribe. I've been away for far too long as it is. I yearn to take her with me, but … it might not be safe for her with my tribe. It might not even be safe for me any longer.

"I wish you well," I say, touching my knuckle to my forehead in the traditional orcish way. "And I will take my leave."

I walk a few steps when I hear the sound I was hoping for.

"Wait."

PAIGE

The word scarcely leaves my lips, and I wonder if it's a mistake.

I mean, an orc leaving is a good thing, or it's supposed to be. This one didn't try to kill or enslave us, though. In fact, both Laney and I owe our lives to him.

Still, he was leaving us, which is as rare as water in the desert. Maybe I should leave well enough alone, but I already said it, and now he's turning around.

He's an unusual looking orc. Slimmer than most with a sleek musculature and long limbs that move with liquid grace. His eyes have more of an almond shape than most orcs I've seen, too, and his hair has a splash of white at the temples though I don't think he's all that old.

His hair is pulled back into a tight topknot, baring his face to the first twinkling stars winking into existence overhead.

Now, I've always sort of secretly thought orcs weren't as monstrous as other humans do. In fact, I kind of think they're aesthetically pleasing. Some of them were even attractive.

This one definitely qualifies as hot, that's for damn sure. I've never seen so much definition on a body before. He's like a Greek god chiseled out of stone.

He's staring at me with dark purple eyes. What should I say to him? I told him to wait.

"I …" Why is my mouth so dry all of a sudden? "I want to thank you."

He nods. "No need."

That's all he says, but he doesn't turn to leave. He remains, an inscrutable light in his lavender eyes.

"Where, uh, where are you going?"

"Back to my tribe. I've been away too long."

Well, that makes sense. He's clearly not with the Red Wyrm Clan. Suddenly I have an impulse to ask him to take us along. I don't know why other than the fact that he fought bravely and well to save us ... and asked for nothing in return.

Surely his tribe can't be all that bad ...

"Please," I say before I lose my nerve, "take us with you."

He startles, his mouth falling open with surprise. I don't think he expected to hear that, yet ... I get the impression that he's not disappointed.

"The journey is a hard one," he replies. "Fraught with perils that make a handful of poorly trained orcs seem like a walk in a meadow."

Poorly trained? Fuck me, those orcs were elite troops as far as I was concerned. Then again, this guy took them out one by one, and he only has a couple of scrapes, including the one over his eye that makes him look like he's wearing face paint.

"It's dangerous everywhere if you're a human." I heft Laney's body in my arms and struggle to my feet. "Please, my sister and I, we don't have anything left to us any longer. The orcs ... that is, the other orcs burned our wagon."

His eyes dart to the pile of ash that used to carry everything we had. A low grunt escapes his throat, seemingly non-committal. Yet his eyes teem with frustration at the wastefulness of his kin.

"Humans do dwell among the Shattered Rock tribe." His voice is a granite growl as if he's trying to intimidate me into abandoning this clearly foolhardy idea. "But that does not mean their lot is an easy one. Humans work to provide food for the orcs, who in turn protect the humans."

"It sounds better than slavery," I say and mean it. "Look, I'm not afraid of hard work, and neither is Laney. She can do a lot for a ten-year-old. She can weave, sew, carve, and craft almost as well as an adult."

I'm trying to sell him on Laney, so he doesn't leave her behind. Nothing about this kind orc has told me that he's going to do any such thing, but you never know.

"I did not say I was unwilling." His eyes narrow slightly. "I needed you to be aware that it is not a safe nor an easy journey and what will be expected of you once you arrive at our tribal lands."

"I understand."

"Then I will take you with me."

My heart leaps with excitement, not to mention relief. Taking care of Laney on my own wouldn't be impossible, but it would be arduous.

"Thank you. I really appreciate this, not to mention you saving us." I offer my hand to him.

"My name is Paige. You already know Laney's name. What's yours?"

"I am Jovak, called the Longstrider by my people."

A slight snarl twitches at his lips when he gives his nickname. For some reason, I think he might not be fond of it.

"I can see why they call you that. You have some seriously long legs, like a giraffe."

"Giraffe?" He tilts his head to the side.

"They aren't native to this continent. Like a really, really tall deer with a long neck." How do you describe a giraffe to someone who's never seen one? Hell, I've never seen one either, except in the picture books Gramps salvaged from before the invasion.

"I see." He looks at my sister and shakes his head. "She will not be able to walk for several days at least. I propose we take the Wyrm tribe's wagon to replace the one you lost."

"Well, we'd have to get the cage off it first."

His eyes flash, and he goes over to the cage, grabbing it with his big, meaty paws. My first thought is that there is no way he is going to move that cage all by himself.

Then, he gives a grunt and the considerable

muscles in his back flex. The cage flips end over end and crashes hard on the other side, deforming enough that the barred door no longer closes.

The two of us load up the jerky and hardtack bread onto the now empty wagon. Then I scavenge what linen I can find ... it's hard to find a scrap of fabric not burned or stained with blood ... I create a little pallet for Laney.

We lay her down, and I stare at her pale face for a long moment. What if she doesn't wake up? Or what if she has brain damage? That orc struck her viciously.

"Do not be afraid."

I whip my gaze around to Jovak. He gestures at my sister.

"I have seen many head injuries. Your sister should make a full recovery. And the shamans can help her if she does not. You will see."

He's trying to make me feel better. My heart does this fluttery thing, and I find myself nodding and trying not to gush all over him.

As far as I'm concerned, Jovak should just tattoo a big red S on his chest because he's acting like my personal superhero.

"The sun has long since set," Jovak says. "It

would be safer to make our journey in the morning, however ..."

He looks at the battlefield and, in particular, the Wyrm tribe orcs he has slain.

"I think we should be away at once and put as much distance between us and this carnage as possible."

"I couldn't agree more."

I'm not sure what happened to our onager. She appears to be long gone. Fortunately, the orcs had their own team, so we utilized them. Jovak surprises me by not getting into the wagon. He walks beside it instead.

Between the rattling of the wagon and the gusty wind, it's almost impossible to carry on a conversation. I spend most of the first few hours of our journey watching patches of moonlight splash over his green skin.

Jovak is so defined and muscular that it almost defies possibility. It's hard to believe he's a real being with those perfect proportions. He's not like most orcs who are pure gristle and brute force. He moves with liquid grace, steady and placid, seemingly as a cat but with eyes like a stalking wolf.

He's trying to hide it, but Jovak is anxious. Perhaps he worries about more of the Wyrm tribe catching up to us. If he's worried, I'm worried. Fortunately, I can distract myself with indecent thoughts about his uniquely chiseled body ….

Nobody has to know. Not even Laney, and especially not Jovak. It would probably make him uncomfortable. Maybe it wouldn't. No, no point crossing the line between fantasy and reality. Reality never lives up to fantasy anyway. Not that I would know, being a novice in the fleshly pursuits.

We travel through the night, and only when the pink heralds of dawn streak the sky does he call for a halt. Jovak leads the team of mules behind a thick copse of trees, a good distance from the rutted road.

I take it upon myself to take care of the onager team. They're cranky from having had to walk all night, but some oats spilled out onto the fresh green grass calms their persnickety mood. I pat the rump of the larger of the two and check on Laney.

She was in and out of consciousness last night. Now she's sleeping, but her slumber seems far more peaceful than it had been before. I hope Jovak is right and she's going to make a full recovery.

Jovak sits on a tree stump and sharpens his metal-hafted ax.

"I will take first watch. You may sleep peacefully."

Watch? I guess he means one of us is going to watch the camp. It makes sense. I've never set a watch, ever. A shiver runs down my spine when I realize how many times someone could have snuck up on Laney and me while we were asleep.

"What's wrong?" he asks, noticing my reaction. "Are you cold?"

The day is warm. There's no way I could be cold. If anyone should be cold, it's him since he's barely dressed.

"No, I'm not cold. I'm just thinking of how vulnerable I've left myself over the years that Laney and I have been on the road."

He stops sharpening his ax and gives me a startled look.

"You've been on the road for years? Just the two of you?"

"For the most part, yeah." I shrug. "I mean, we've taken up with roving bands of humans before, but sooner or later, I need to get my space, you know?"

"Your ... space?" He tilts his head to the side and considers me for a long moment.

"Uh, well, it's complicated." Suddenly my

cheeks burn with shame. I don't want to admit this to him, and it's downright silly.

"And you think I can't understand complicated things?"

Oh great, now I've insulted him. Now I *have* to tell him what I mean.

"I guess ..." my voice breaks, and I clear my throat. "I guess that I get sort of uncomfortable in those bands after a while."

I scratched the back of my head and turned my gaze down on the sleeping Laney. I bunched up the blankets into a humped mound to keep the sun off her face.

"I mean, the men always want to lay claim to me sooner or later, and it causes problems that I don't want to settle down with anyone."

"You don't want a mate?" He seems somewhat astonished by the idea.

"I guess I haven't wanted to, uh ..." I almost said *I don't want to mate with the men I've met so far.* "I guess I haven't wanted to mate with any of them, at any rate."

He grunts as if he understands.

"I, too, do not wish to take a mate." A scowl crosses his face. "My folk have been pushing me to do so for some time. It seems like a complication I do not need."

"Yeah, it's complicated, all right," I agree, though it's not like I've ever really been in a relationship either.

Thunder crackles in the sky. I look upward and see the blue patch of sunny skies over us was going to be a temporary condition. Ominous-looking clouds amass in the east, flashing with lightning.

"Feel the storm?" He rises and stares at nature's brewing fury. "It's coming."

6

JOVAK

Thunder cracks the sky, and lightning fractures the clouds as I hasten to rig up a tent using the wagon and salvaged tarps. The fabric has an oiled backing, making them water resistant, but attaching them in a way the wind won't tear them away is a chore.

The wagon we appropriated from the Wyrm clan features metal hasps where the cage could be chained into place. By cutting strategic slits in the tarp, I manage to secure it with the help of sticks and leather straps. A stick goes through the rounded hasp, and twine holds it in place.

The wind is really picking up, sending my topknot out straight behind me during the stiffest gusts. Paige squints as the wind blows dust into her face, her arms laden with another tarp.

"I scavenged this from an old campsite down the road."

"Good," I say, throwing it over the one remaining gap. "Well done."

Her lips stretch in a cautious smile. It makes her even lovelier if that were possible. I try not to stare, but it's difficult. The last thing I want is to make her uncomfortable.

Why, though? When she first asked to come along, I tried to convince her how dangerous the journey would truly be. Yet, I was happy when she decided to take the risk anyway.

She helps me to secure the final tarp in place as drops of rain spatter down. One lands on my forehead, and it's surprisingly cold.

"Paige?"

The weak voice comes from within the wagon. Paige gasps and hurries under the tarp to check on her sister. I remain outside, finishing the work of protecting us from the rain.

By the time I finish, the rain has become a steady hiss. The cold drops put a chill on my skin, but it would be worse if I were human. I climb into the wagon with the humans, careful to crowd my body into the farthest end from them.

Inside the tarps, it's next to pitch black. Only a weak light diffuses through the gridwork stitching of the tarps. Once the fabric grows damp and sags with the rain, it allows in even less light.

The wind tears at the tarp, but our bindings hold, at least for now. A bit of water leaks through a gap, but fortunately, it is right over a hole in the wagon bed, so most of it goes right back out.

"Paige," Laney says in a weak voice. "That man is an orc."

"Yes, he is, but he's not going to hurt you. He's been helping us."

In the half-light, I can dimly make out Paige's freckled face turning my way. I think she's smiling, but it's hard to tell.

"Why?"

Laney's question hangs in the air like an intangible pall.

"What do you mean?" Paige asks at length with a nervous half-laugh.

"Why would an orc help us? You said they were all bad."

Even in the darkness, I know Paige's face flushes with embarrassment.

"I never said *all* orcs were bad," Paige says hastily. "I just said that we should be careful around them, just in case they were bad."

Paige clears her throat and looks over at me again.

"Uh, maybe it would help if you introduced yourself, Jovak."

"Hello, Laney," I say in as pleasant a tone as I can manage. "My name is Jovak. I am … friends with your sister."

"If you hurt my sister, I'll kill you," Laney says, utterly deadpan.

"Laney," Paige gasps in horror. "That's not polite."

"I mean it, though."

"I have no doubt that you do, little one," I interject. "I will not allow harm to come to you or your sister so long as it's within my power to prevent it."

I had meant for it to be a fierce declaration, but then I lost confidence as I spoke. Neither human seems to notice or comment if they do.

"Is it raining, Paige?" Laney asks.

"Yes, it's raining hard," Paige replies.

"What happened to the orcs who tried to take us prisoner?"

"They're not a problem any longer," Paige

replies, shooting what I assume to be a grateful smile my way. I can't really tell in the dark, but her tone suggests so.

"Does that mean that Jovak killed them all?"

"Well," Paige says, clearing her throat.

"I killed them all, Laney," I reply, not without some pride.

"Good," Laney says, her voice thick with approaching slumber. Soon she's snoring softly again. I try to sleep as well, but the raging storm and general feeling of unease prevent me from achieving even a modicum of rest.

Eventually, the rain dies to a light drizzle, and the thunder cracks grow more and more faint as the storm moves westward. Though thoughts of Paige and her sister are distracting, particularly Paige. I start to relax.

I'm not sure what it is, but there's something I find unusually appealing about her. It's not just the obvious, her physical beauty. There's something more. Perhaps it is her intelligence and bravery. Or maybe it's because she's easy to talk to. The life of a chief is a lonely one. Even my sister, the one person I can rely on in the tribe not to speak ill of me, can't really speak freely with me.

Paige is removed from the tribe, so maybe I feel

safer conversing with her. I only know that I look forward to when she awakes, and we can talk more. I'm fascinated to know more about her and where she and her sister come from.

A snapping twig brings me out of my half-slumber. It could have been a stick barely holding on through the storm, which just now fell from the high limbs of the trees … but I don't think so.

My nostrils test the air and detect a thick, musky aroma. I thrust my head through the canopy and saw a large, shaggy form, like a miniature hill, moving through our camp. The onagers awaken and begin making distressed sounds.

It's something the humans call a bear. The orc word for the beast translates into *grumpy, furry, teeth, and claws.*

I can't allow it to harm Paige, or our onager team, for that matter. They are fearsome foes.

But so am I.

I throw the tarp open fully and leap out the back, brandishing both of my axes and giving a ferocious war cry. Sometimes you can scare bears off by acting loud and threatening. Not this time, it seems. The bear turns its head my way and growls in annoyance.

"You will find no meals here," I shout back. "Begone with you, beast."

The bear rises onto its hind legs. An intimidation display and an effective one. It must stand more than ten feet tall, from its clawed feet to the top of its furry head.

I roar and charge. The metal-hafted ax bites deep into its flank. The bear gives a bellow and drops to all fours, running away fast under iron-gray skies.

I bend down and grab a handful of leaves to clean the blood and fur from my blade, then re-sheathe my ax. I turn to the wagon and find Paige staring right at me. Her eyes are full of wonder.

"I can't believe you stood up to an actual bear," she says. "That thing was huge."

"I could not let it harm you or the child."

What I said, I spoke matter of fact. It was not calculated to impress, and yet Paige's eyes shine with meaning as soon as I utter the words.

"Jovak, you're ... you're really great."

She flushes red, her freckles vanishing amid a sea of scarlet skin. I find a smile coming to my lips.

"My tribe does not always think so, but I appreciate the words."

"Well, I'll be sure to tell your tribe when we

meet them how awesome their chief is. How about that?"

I chuckle. "If you like."

She peers out the tarp at the sky and frowns. "I think there's more rain on the way. It looks like we're stuck here for tonight."

"Hopefully, the bear will be the only thing to trouble us during our stay."

"Yeah, no shit."

I frown. "What?"

"Oh, it's a human thing. It means, 'yeah, you're right.' The opposite of being full of shit."

Full of shit is a human phrase I have heard before. I chuckle lightly, but the truth is I'm worried. We did not get far from the battlefield, where I had left six Wyrm orcs dead.

The interior of the wagon falls silent as we both try to return to slumber. After a time, she sighs and sits up.

"I don't think I can sleep."

"I cannot either," I reply.

"Well, we could talk to pass the time."

"Indeed. I would be interested in hearing of your exploits, Paige. You and your sister have been on a remarkable journey."

"Remarkable," she snickers. "Yeah, that's a word for it. So is terrifying."

She tells me about some of her travels. It sounds as if she's been moving around for a long time. One thing that she never seems to mention is where her home was. Her journey started somewhere.

Dawn breaks and brings an end to the rain at last. The road proves much too muddy for the wagon's wheels, however.

"I guess we're stuck here until it dries out," she says.

"I do not like this area. It is too exposed, and it's clearly part of a bear's hunting ground. We should look for better shelter if we have to spend another night in this area."

I start a slow, spiraling path away from the wagon, trying to keep it in sight. When that fails, I try to keep it in earshot. I'm ranging a bit farther out than I wanted to when I finally spot it ... an old, decrepit, but reasonably intact human dwelling constructed from the felled trunks of trees.

I get behind the wagon and push it through the mud until we reach the cabin. The onager team isn't happy about it, but they pull the load with only a few braying complaints, thanks to my help.

I'm covered with sweat by the time I finish. She takes care of the mule team and tends to her sister while I investigate the small cabin. The inside seems more intact than the outside. I doubt the various dusty cans contain anything edible on the shelves, but there is game in the woods for us to eat.

I search far and wide for enough dry firewood for the hearth. On the way back, I realized that I had pushed things a bit too far with the wagon. My shoulder twinges with pain. I grimace but don't drop my load until I get the wood safely inside the cabin.

"What's wrong?" Paige asks. She looks up from where she sits beside Laney. She had laid the child on a battered sofa and covered her. Laney appears to be sleeping peacefully.

"A light strain."

I sit in front of the hearth and rub the knotted muscles as best I can. I draw out some pasty unguent that our shamans make that's good for muscle cramps and smear it on, but the most sensitive spot remains out of reach.

"Here."

I look up to find Paige there, holding her hand out.

"Let me help."

After a moment's hesitation, I place the substance in her hand. She goes behind me and rubs it on the sore spot, finding it with unerring accuracy. I groan as she works on the cramp with surprisingly strong hands.

"You're too tense," she says. "Try to relax."

Relax? When her every touch sends fires shooting through my skin? My heart thuds hard, rushing blood through my ears. It's all I can do not to cry out.

"There you go," she says, wiping the excess paste on her own skin. "I don't know what's in this stuff, but it's so soothing."

"Thank you."

I rise from the floor, preparing to build a fire at last. When I reach down to pick up a log, her hand also falls on it.

"Oh," she says. "I guess we both had the same idea, huh?"

I look up. Her face is inches away, her breath warm on my skin. Paige's blue eyes shine with … something. Something I cannot name. Or dare not.

Before I can think about it twice, I lean forward and sweetly kiss her plump lips.

7

PAIGE

God, I was so hoping he'd kiss me.

Now that he has, I'm utterly overwhelmed by the pulses of fire racing through my veins. His lips on my own are pure magic. I find myself relaxing into the kiss, exulting in the taste of his lips.

Jovak's hands come up to my face, caressing my cheeks. His hands are huge and practically envelop my head, but I don't care. Not as long as he keeps kissing me like this.

His tongue slips into my mouth, and a moan escapes my throat. Our breath mingles as I lash my tongue against his. Lips smack, tongues play, and our mutual hearts beat only a few inches from each other.

Jovak dropped one hand from my face and slid it down my back. I leaned into him harder, my pulse a thudding tympany in my ears. It doesn't matter that I'm inexperienced. I seem to be doing it right. He's enjoying himself or doing a damn good fakery of it.

Oh god, where is this going? Stupid question. It's pretty obvious where it's going. Even before his hand slides down my back until his lowest finger just brushes the slope of my ass. A pulse like fire shoots through me, and I feel my body responding to his touch, his kiss, his manly musk-like scent.

I feel my entire nervous system being doused in electricity. It feels so damn good to be kissing him. Is *this* what I was missing? The older girls under-sold this experience, if anything. I feel as if we're floating on a cloud.

Only we're not floating. My sister is sleeping not far away. That thought should probably make me stop, or at least slow down, but I can't bring myself to stop kissing Jovak long enough for that to happen.

A hard lump presses against me from right between his legs. I know what that is, and I know what it means. Part of me wants to go all the way.

Okay, I'll be honest. Most of me wants to go all the way.

But Laney … and I get the feeling that if we give in to our passions and let them sweep us away, it will get … loud.

Maybe it's a good thing my sister is here. Maybe it's best if we just stop. Where is this going? He already said he doesn't want a mate. And even if he did, nothing says he wants that mate to be me. After all, he's a chieftain. He's probably going to mate with an orc who happens to be a chieftain's daughter.

What chance would we really have? While I ache for him, burn for him, I know this is doomed from the start.

Not only that, but it feels *too* good. I don't know if I'm supposed to enjoy it this much. I have no basis for comparison at all, considering the fact that this is my first time. If the actual sex is supposed to be better than this, then I'm afraid I will lose all control.

I stop kissing him back, stiffening in his arms. He stops right away, pulling back enough to meet my gaze.

"What's the matter?" he asks softly. Oh god, I don't want to hurt his feelings. The last thing I want is to drive this strangely noble and kind orc away from me. He's the first man to be good to me and my sister since Gramps died.

And yet, I can't let myself go and just flow with the moment. There's something else gnawing at me, a tiny voice in my head telling me that this good feeling is just the setup for a great big fall.

Every other time I've let myself be happy, every other time I've given in to just enjoying myself, it's ended in tragedy or disaster. Every single time. Good feelings are just illusions, traps to lure you into a false sense of security.

Then life shovels shit in your face.

"Paige?" My name is a velvety soft whisper on his tongue. "What's the matter? Did I hurt you?"

Hurt me? Ha! It would be easier if he had. No, Jovak, you didn't hurt me, but I don't know what to say.

His eyes contain such tenderness, mingled with steamy desire, that it's too much for me. I have to get away. It's not like I can have him. Not really. Not in a lasting way that really matters.

"I'm sorry," I say, the words like lead on my tongue. I put my hands on his chest and then pushed away. He lets me go without a fight, his hands extending to the side.

"Have I done something wrong?" The look of hurtful rejection in his eyes is too much to bear. I know how much he wants me … almost as much as I want him. We've been feeling this tension climb ever since he saved our lives in the valley.

I shook my head because I couldn't hope to speak over the choking, gasping sob trying to work its way out of my throat. I just can't swallow it down.

"I'm scared," I managed to croak out at last as the tears began to fall. They slid down my cheeks, hot and bothersome, adding to the frustration taking hold of me.

With that, I have to run. Even though there could be orcs, bears, or worse, in the woods, I flee into the dusk.

I moved into the tree line, my vision blurring with tears. My shoulders and chest shake with heavy sobs. I don't know why I'm crying. I don't know quite why I ran away, and I don't know why I can't bring myself to go back to him. It's probably best if I don't, but I want to.

I hear the door open again and then his heavy tread. I turned around and pressed my forehead into the rough bark of a tree, tears continuing to fall. It's so unfair. I want to give in to my desires, but I feel too much fear to let myself. Surely anything that feels this good must be a trick.

The leaves crunched underfoot as Jovak came around the trunk of the tree. I can't bear to look at him. He might be furious with me. Maybe he thinks I'm a tease or something. I don't know, but I'm afraid he's going to leave Laney and me behind now. After all, I rejected him and ran away.

"Paige …"

His voice carries no hint of recrimination. Only worry and a desire to soothe me. His hand falls on my shoulder, and I start sobbing harder.

"What's wrong?"

I don't know how to tell him. I can't even put all of these fractured thoughts and feelings into a semblance of order. I roil inside and out, riding the waves of powerful emotions I have stymied for so very long.

He gently pulled my shoulder. I allowed him to turn me around, but I kept my hands pressed over my face.

"Paige."

He took me into his arms, gently this time. This isn't torrid passion. It's his desire to comfort. I fell into him, crying harder than ever, and buried my face in his chest.

"I'm sorry," I say between wracking sobs. "I'm so sorry."

"Shhh," he says softly, petting my hair exactly the way I do Laney's when she's upset.

"You're probably going to leave us now," I say in a wail. "Please don't leave us. We've been alone for so long, I don't know if I …"

I can't form articulate speech when I'm crying this hard. I don't think I've cried like this since Gramps died … if I even did it then.

"No," he says firmly, still petting my hair. "I won't leave you, either of you."

That should be reassuring, and indeed it is. But good feelings ironically instill fear and anxiety in me. So naturally, I start crying even harder.

"I won't abandon you," he says again. "I said I would take you to my tribe, and I will do so. I do not go back on my word. Unless I'm trying to deceive a damned pointy-eared dark elf."

When he mentions dark elves, the vitriol in his voice is tinged with … something. I'm not sure what. Something beyond simple prejudice or hatred. I file the thought away for later since I'm hardly in any shape to ask him about it. Besides, now is not the time.

"It would not speak highly of my character if I

left you two to your fate just because you rejected my advances," he says. There's disappointment in his voice but no anger or bitterness. I can't stand to make him feel this way.

"I'm not rejecting you," I say quickly, looking up at him through eyes still misty with tears. It occurs to me that I probably look like shit. "Oh god," I say, pulling away from him somewhat, though his arms remain on my shoulders. "I must look awful, all covered with snot and my face swollen …."

"No," he says, his eyes wide and tender. "No, my sweet Paige. You are beautiful. You will always be beautiful to me."

I don't know why, but I needed to hear that, put that way specifically. My crying subsided, though the occasional sob still racks my body.

"You've been kinder to me than anyone I've met since I left home," I mumble. It's hard, but I force myself to lift my gaze and meet his own. "I'm so sorry."

"You have nothing to apologize for."

Maybe not, but I feel like I do.

"Jovak, I … when it comes to you and me … can you give me time? Please? Just some time to sort … to sort all of this out in my head?"

He nods. "Of course, Paige. I will give you anything you want or need."

Jovak pulls me back into his embrace, and I willingly go with the motion. I wrap my arms around him and hold on tight, so very tight.

He won't abandon us. He says he'll wait for me.

I feel it's far more than I deserve, but I'll take it.

8

JOVAK

I held Paige in the moonlight for a long time after she stopped crying. My hands slid over her back, from time to time, in an attempt to make her feel more comfortable. It's hard to hold my desires in check, no pun intended. Yet I manage to do so.

I want her so badly that I almost can't stand it. I burn for her more than I have for any female in my entire life. When she pushed away from me and fled, I had a dark moment where I wanted to be angry with her for rejecting me.

Fortunately, the moment passed, and I was able to push through it. When I went after her, it was out of concern for her well-being.

I was prepared to get used to the idea of being

disappointed, but then she said something that gave me hope.

She said it wasn't a rejection, and she asked me for time. Time? I have only just met this woman, and yet I feel like I would wait for her until the moon fell out of the sky.

I held her for a long time and then gently guided her back toward the cabin. Once we got inside, I laid her down on the bedding near her sister. She was asleep before I even covered her up.

I built a fire in the hearth and then sat beside its crackling warmth. I always found a fire to be soothing. Pity, she's asleep and can't enjoy it with me. Then again, maybe it's best she rests. We have a hard journey ahead of us.

I watched her sleep for a long time until my own eyelids grew heavy. I fell into a deep slumber and didn't awaken until after the sun was well in the sky the next day.

Paige and I didn't talk about what happened the night before, but we did speak. It's mostly about practical matters like breaking camp and preparing to head north toward my people's lands, but the easy and carefree manner in which we speak gives me hope. Hope that maybe she'll come around.

It seems I must woo her. Strange because I've never done any such thing before. I have had many lovers, but this is different. This feels like it needs to be more than just a one-night tryst or even an extended torrid affair. This feels … right, but it's happening too fast. I never thought I would be in this situation. I had pushed all thoughts of taking a mate from my mind.

Yet, that's all I can think about when I'm around her. Making her my mate, and the act of mating her itself ….

We packed up the wagon and began our journey anew. The sun has dried out the road by early afternoon, and we are making good time rattling along. Paige and I talk and share the occasional laugh about the bear that came calling to our camp and the caprice of nature in general.

After the end of the second day on the road, Laney has recovered almost fully. I've never seen anyone spring back from injury so quickly. While we are making camp beside a babbling brook, Paige headed off into the woods by herself for a bit, and I'm left with Laney.

"So," Laney says, fixing me with her too-wise-for-her-age gaze. "Alone at last, huh?" I'm not sure what she means. She notices my quizzical frown and elaborates. "I mean, you like my sister, don't you?"

My head pops up, and I give her a hard stare. "I'm not sure these are the types of matters to be discussed with children."

Laney rolls her eyes, and I feel foolish for some reason. "I'm ten, not five. Paige told me about the birds and the bees."

"What do feathers and stingers have to do with it?" I shake my head. "You're talking in riddles. Yes, I like your sister. She is brave, kind, and lovely, but we don't have … that kind of relationship."

"Maybe not," she says, her eyes narrowing. "But that's what you both want. I can tell."

"I'm not sure either of us wants that."

"You're not a very good liar, Jovak Longstrider," Laney says. "But you're a pretty good guy, you know that?"

I snarl at her. "I am a warrior whose blades have spilled enough blood to fill a river, youngling. I do not think I am a 'good guy' by your human standards."

Laney laughs at me. "The hell with that. You're a good guy. I can tell. I have a sense for these kinds of things."

Her hand goes to her head, and she grimaces.

"Another headache?"

"Yes, but it's not as bad as the one I had yesterday." She's in pain, but she seems intent on forging through it. "Listen, my sister is pretty standoffish. You're not the first man to try to sweep her off of her feet."

"Indeed?" Now I'm rapt with attention. If I find out why she rejected her past suitors, it will help me understand what she wants in a man. Then I can woo her accordingly.

"Oh yeah, lots of guys want her." Laney shrugs. "She's beautiful, smart, and tough."

"Why did she reject the others?"

"I don't know," she said with a shrug. "I know that she's super picky, but it's more than that. I think she's afraid that if she really cares about someone, even loves them, that something bad is going to happen."

"That would seem to me to be an irrational fear."

Laney blows a razz and snorts. "Yeah, no kidding, but it's how she feels. The good news is all of those guys were missing something. The secret ingredient."

I arch my brows in query. "Secret ... ingredient? What kind of secret ingredient?"

"Moi," she says, gesturing to herself.

"Moi?" I repeat the strange word, gesturing at myself. "Is this some kind of word of power for a human love spell?"

Laney laughs really hard, almost falling out of the wagon. Only the fact that her head starts bothering her interrupts her exuberant mirth.

"Ow," she says, grimacing and rubbing her head. "No, it's not a spell. Moi means 'me' in another language. I forget the name, but Laney says it sometimes. I think she picked it up from our grampa before he died."

"You're the secret ingredient?"

"Sure," Laney said. "I didn't like any of those other guys. And just between you and me, nobody stands a chance of winning Paige's heart without me liking them."

"I appreciate and value your support, little one," I reply.

"Good, because you should." She sticks her tongue out at me. "With me in your corner, you can't lose."

I laughed at her childish exuberance, but I got the feeling she was dead serious too. She held her fist out toward me. I stared at it curiously for a moment.

"You're supposed to fist bump," she says with a sigh, tapping her knuckles into my own. Her hand is so tiny compared to mine, but I appreciate the sentiment.

About that time, her sister returned, and our conversation was over. But Laney sticks true to her word. For the next few days, as we travel the long and winding road back to Shattered Rock lands, Laney drops subtle and some not-so-subtle clues that she thinks I would be the perfect man for Paige.

I appreciate her efforts, yet it's kind of embarrassing. Mostly for Paige, whose face turns red almost every time Laney mentions it.

Yet Laney is far from fully recovered and spends a lot of time resting or sleeping in the wagon. This gives Paige and me plenty of time to talk. Most of the things we speak of aren't important at all. Some are very important. But one thing always remains true ... we spend most of our time smiling.

In fact, at the end of one particularly long day, my cheeks hurt from smiling so much, and my throat was a bit raw from laughter. I drink honey mixed with milk to help my throat, but I suppose it's a good problem to have, laughing yourself sore.

Then, on the seventh day after I rescued her, we came upon a totem. A stack of stones waist high to me are piled on top of each other until the shadow crosses over the road ahead of us. The stones are painted with white sigils and fearsome-looking faces.

"Um," Paige says as we move past the marker. "That's not exactly welcoming."

"Believe it or not, that is a good sign. That marker was left by my people. It signifies we are passing into my tribe's territory."

"Oh," she says, relaxing a little. "Good."

She noticed that I didn't relax as much as her, and she frowned.

"I mean, is it good? You seem kind of tense, Jovak. Or is it your shoulder again? You want me to rub it for you?"

"No, it's not my shoulder," I say quickly, even though the idea of her hands on my body in any capacity is an enticing one. "I'm just ... alert. On the edge of readiness."

She nods, but I can tell she knows there's more to it than that. The truth is, I'm a bit wary of the very tribe I lead. I'm not sure how they will react to me being gone for so long, much less what they will think of my taking in two human refugees upon my return.

As we venture deeper into Shattered Rock lands, I become aware of presences. I can't make them out. I can't see, hear, or even smell them, but I know my tribe is watching us from afar. They hide in the trees, behind grassy knolls, and in the depressions left by dry riverbeds. Watching and waiting.

I hadn't expected a warm welcome, but neither did I expect to be stalked. If not for Laney and Paige, I would have already stopped and demanded that my people show themselves. I don't want to risk a confrontation, however. Not with the chance of the two humans being hurt.

"Is it just me," Paige says, her eyes narrowing cautiously, "or does it feel like we're being watched?"

"It's not just you," I respond in a low growl. My head is on a swivel as I spin my gaze this way and that. They're close now, very close. I still can't see them, but now I can smell them. I hear things too. The whisk of a leather sole on a rock upthrust from the dirt. The gentle shake of a leaf as a large body moves past. A sharp intake of breath as someone ducks behind a tree trunk right before I spot them.

Then, they make their move.

A dozen orcs melt out of the woods, all of them with bows drawn and arrows nocked. I tried to shield Paige with my body and drew my axes.

"Get down," I growl to Paige as I turn this way and that, trying to keep track of all of them at once and failing miserably.

My eyes narrow to slits, and I stand straight, letting the axes droop to my sides.

"Is this how you greet your chieftain?" I snap. "With weapons drawn and eyes filled with hate?"

An orc loosens his bow, letting it go slack. He walks in front of the others, lips twitching in a snarl. He's almost as tall as me and built like a boulder.

Rolar. The most vocal of my critics in the tribe and the last one of them that I wanted to meet on the road.

"You cannot be our chief," Rolar growls. "After all, you are a dead man."

9

PAIGE

’m too scared to breathe.

Orcs melted out of the woods like magic, surrounding us with arrows drawn and nocked. I hear the tendons of the archers, as well as the bent, springy wood of their bows creaking. I've seen an orcish bow put an arrow through a tree trunk before.

Grandpa taught me how to hunt using a bow with a thirty-pound pull, sufficient for most game. But orcs use bows with a minimum ... a minimum ... of one hundred pounds. Most humans would struggle just to string such a bow, but there are a dozen of them aimed our way now.

No, not our way. Only at Jovak. The orc who spoke isn't quite as tall as Jovak, but he's twice as big around. What he lacks in grace he clearly makes up for in raw bulk and muscle. He has a scar on his cheek that makes him look like he has a perpetual sneer. Or maybe he just has a perpetual sneer, and the scar is incidental.

Whatever the case, I don't like him. I feel hostility coming off of him in palpable waves. From all the orcs, really, but mostly from him. I get the feeling he's something of a rival for Jovak. Maybe someone who wants the chieftainship bad enough to kill for it.

I shift in the wagon, not sure what I should do or say. It's a volatile situation, and the slightest thing could set it off like a bomb. I don't want to be the reason Jovak gets killed. He's done so much for me already, and I've had scant chances to pay him back.

Jovak still has his axes in hand and is ready to send them flying at a moment's notice. I have no doubt he'd hit his targets, too, and probably kill them. But that would leave ten other orcs to stick him full of arrows like a pincushion.

Jovak seems to have the same assessment of the situation I do. He casts a glance back at me, and his eyes are filled with worry. I feel bad for him. Once again, I'm getting in the way. If he were alone, perhaps he would stand a chance against these orcs. Probably not, but I still feel like an anchor around his neck.

He straightens, losing his fighting stance in lieu of towering over the orc who apparently leads this band of archers.

"I always thought that one day you would take your shot at me, Rolar. But in my imagination, you were enough of an orc and a warrior to do it one-on-one. Not relying on a team of archers like a coward."

The apparent Rolar snorts with derision, relaxing his posture a bit more.

"You fling accusations like a dog flinging water after running in the rain. I am not making threats, Jovak."

"Chief Jovak," Jovak snaps. The gathered orcs exchange glances, and one by one, they let out the tautness of their bows. I notice they still have their arrows nocked, though. It wouldn't be hard for them to take aim and fire. We're not out of the woods yet.

"As I said, you cannot be the chief because you are dead. When you did not return, the council decided to declare you officially dead."

"I've only been gone a matter of days," Jovak says.

"You have been gone for over a moon."

Rolar's voice holds a definite note of accusation. His feelings are hurt, I realize. All of them have some mixture of betrayal and contempt on their faces.

Jovak looks surprised to hear him speak.

"Surely it has not been so long as that," Jovak says, but I hear the lack of confidence in his voice. "Has it?"

His voice trails off, and his eyes seem distant. I assume he's recalling the time in his head. When he finishes, the look of dread in his eyes lets me know that Rolar's estimate isn't far off. That does seem like a very long time for a leader to be away from his people.

"Yes, I can see it in your eyes, 'Chief' Jovak," Rolar says with disgust. "And while you have been off cavorting in distant lands, our people have suffered."

Jovak's eyes grow hard and serious.

"What are you speaking of, Rolar? Tell me this instant and cease your cryptic ways."

Rolar's scarred face twists into a smirk

"You would have me speak plainly, my Chief?"

he snorts. "Very well. In the last fortnight, we've lost seven tribesmen. Vanished without a trace."

"Vanished?" Jovak's gaze narrows. "Surely there must be some signs of where they went missing, at the least."

"Of the seven who went missing, three were on the same patrol route. The others were ranging in totally different directions." Rolar stops posturing for a moment, and the two seem to be on the same page. "We have found no pattern in any of it. Not all of our tribesmen who patrol are going missing, yet it's a constant worry."

Jovak shook his head.

"Why did you not start patrolling in pairs after the first few of them went missing?"

"We did that after the first two were gone," Rolar snapped. "We are not so stupid as to be helpless without a chief."

"If I'm so unnecessary, then why are you all so upset about my long absence?"

Rolar snarled.

"Without the chief to give the final word, our people bicker among each other about the right course of action to take. We have been stymied by indecision. Eventually, I gathered these brave warriors together, and we set out to search for our missing brethren ourselves."

Jovak nods, and there's a measure of respect in his eyes and in his tone when he speaks.

"A wise decision. I approve."

It's subtle, but Rolar puffs up his chest at the praise from his chief. I take it there's not a total lack of respect between these two. If anything, I'd say that Rolar is more hurt than angry.

"It is not so wise, perhaps, given we have found no sign of them."

"How long have you ranged out?" Jovak asks.

"For the last three days."

"And you have seen no signs of them?" Jovak sheathes his axes and strokes his chin in thought. "There must be a way we can find out what happened to them. Perhaps if we split your band into thirds ..."

"Stop giving orders as if you are the chieftain," Rolar snaps. "At the next full moon, the council will select a new chieftain for the Shattered Rock tribe."

"That is no longer necessary. I am clearly not dead. Only death may release a chieftain from his duties. Be that death by the hands of an enemy or his own people, our laws are clear, Rolar."

Rolar's face grows dark, and his jowls shake with rage when he speaks.

"You are already dead to many of us, Jovak. You do not dwell among those you lead. You choose to be apart from us. No one can get close to you even when you are not on one of your jaunts. It is no wonder you have never taken a mate."

My stomach is tied in knots. I don't like this. I don't like discord, which is part of why I never stayed with the roving bands of humans much. I glanced back into the rear of the wagon. Thankfully my little sister still slumbers. If she were to awaken, she'd probably do something crazy, like try to attack Rolar or something. She and Jovak have gotten quite tight in the last few days.

"Enough." Jovak's powerful chest heaves in a sigh. "You have made your point clear, Rolar. Very well, continue on as you will. I wish you luck and hope you find our missing tribesmen soon."

Rolar flinches. I don't think he expected Jovak to say anything like that. Now he doesn't have any reason to argue, not really. Rolar jerked his head toward the trail.

"Let's go. Surely the Longstrider can find his way back to the tribe. That is if he can remember the way after being gone for so long."

They return to their journey through the forest, most of them refusing to even look at Jovak. More than a few looked my way, though, including Rolar. He gives me a friendly nod and a smile.

"You will be most welcome in our midst, golden hair. Not all orcs wander. Some of us are home with our mates every night."

Well, that was probably the orcish idea of subtlety. He might as well have hung a sign around his neck saying he's available and amenable to mating with me, a human woman.

I'm not interested. I don't know if it's because of the connection I've forged with Jovak or if he's just not my type, but I don't feel the same way for Rolar that I do with the chieftain.

Jovak turned to me with a sheepish expression on his handsome face. I guess my questions are written all over my face because I don't have to say anything. He just starts explaining.

"I am not in good standing with my tribe, it would seem." He heaves a long sigh. "And I can hardly blame them. I have been spending more and more time apart on my journeys. I was not here for them when they really needed me."

"So your tribe is upset with you," I say. "Because you like to ramble?"

"That, and because I have not taken a mate." Jovak can't quite look me in the eyes when he speaks. "With no clear line of succession, the tribe has endured a great deal of strife. Young bucks like Rolar are jockeying for position."

"You …" I swallow hard, "you made it sound earlier like your people challenge for the right of succession."

He nodded, and his chest puffed out just a bit.

"Indeed, but I am my tribe's greatest warrior." He's bragging. I can't believe it. He's trying to sound impressive. I guess this is the orcish way of courtship. I'm flattered, but at the same time, I'm worried about his standing with the tribe. "There are none who believe they could defeat me in a one-on-one battle, and they are correct. Also, they expect me to pass my strength down to the next generation, and one cannot do that without a mate."

Soon he falls silent as we pass another of the totem markers. I see plumes of smoke trailing into the air, and I can smell the telltale signs of civilization. Then I got my first look at the Shattered Rock.

I don't see any shattered rocks around. What I do see is what used to be some sort of outdoor amphitheater, which has become the centerpiece of their settlement. The amphitheater forms a kind of natural shade, cooling the houses that dot the area around it. There's a working mill with a spinning wheel powered by a narrow, but deep and slow-moving, stream. Somewhere there is a blacksmith, at least judging by the sound of hammering, and plenty of people around.

Not just orcs, either. About a third of the population seems to be human.

Rolling fields of grain, corn, and other crops spread out in the distance. These are fertile lands, no wonder the tribe holds onto them so fiercely.

At our approach, a group of orcs clusters around us. No one raises an alarm, they just sort of melt out of the woodwork. And none of them look happy.

"So the Longstrider's not dead after all."

"Might as well be as much good as he does us." That comment is followed up by a fat wad of spittle sent into the dirt.

"Get out of here, Jovak! You abandoned us. You will find no aid here."

"He is not worthy to be on our lands."

"Betrayer!"

"A weak-willed leader with arms too stout for his own good."

An older orc woman dressed in ceremonial feathered robes pushes her way to the front of the crowd. Her wizened face has seen many turns of the seasons, but her eyes are as clear and sharp as a hawk's.

"Shaman Otunga," Jovak says with great respect.

"Where have you been, Chief Jovak?" she snapped with a surprisingly strong voice, despite how heavily she leaned on her gnarled walking stick. "Where have you been while our people have vanished and their loved ones have suffered so? Well? What task was so important that you had to leave us twisting in the wind?"

Shit, this isn't good. I know that Jovak was following the dark elf army at first, but it would have been pretty obvious after at least the second day they were not a threat to his own tribe. After that, he was simply indulging his curiosity and shirking his duties.

They're going to oust him, if not straight up kill him if he tells the truth. This is one angry mob. What can I do? He's helped Laney and me so much.

He literally saved our lives again and again. I have to do something ….

And then it hits me that I do have one card to play, one move to make.

"I'm sorry," I say in my best parade voice. All the gazes that whip my way make me feel anxious, but none more than that of Otunga herself. "It's all my fault he's been away for so long. You see, your chief did not abandon you for some fool's errand. He was claiming a mate."

Gasps rise from the gathered throng. The shaman stares at me so hard I think I'm going to burst into flames.

"And where is this mate?" she asks.

"Right here," I say, putting my hand on Jovak's shoulder as his mouth gaped open. "I'm his mate."

10

JOVAK

I turn my astonished gaze on Paige. Has she gone absolutely mad? What possessed her to say such a thing?

Unless … I am not the most familiar with human courtship rituals. Perhaps she has changed her mind? Perhaps I gave her enough time, and she's made her decision about me? My heart soars at the thought.

Then, she catches my gaze and gives me a subtle wink. So, it is a ruse, then. But why? Does she really think this is going to make things better between the people I lead and me?

Only it seems to be working. The looks of shock are fading, replaced by everything from curiosity to alarm to hope. Otunga narrows her gaze on Paige and takes a crooked step forward.

"What did you say, human?"

Paige blanches a little under Otunga's gaze. There are few who would not, and all of them are insane. But she stiffens her spine and meets the old shaman's gaze spark for spark.

"I said he claimed a mate. Me."

Otunga glances at me, and her lips twitch.

"Is this true, Chief Jovak?"

Her tone is different. She's still angry, but there's a note of hope as well.

"Yes." I wrapped my arm around her body, hand at her waist, and pulled Paige close to my side. "Yes, this is my mate. Allow me to introduce you to Paige the Holdfast."

She glances at me.

"Holdfast?"

"Yes, because you held fast to your ground even when faced with a foe much mightier than yourself." I turn my gaze to my people as they all gasp and exchange incredulous looks. "Yes, that is the right of it. I found my mate in the Valley of Lost Souls many leagues to the south."

"What were you doing so far away as the Valley of Lost Souls?" Otunga demands.

"At first, I was tracking a dark elf army," I reply smoothly as if it's a matter of course. "But soon I began to feel an inexorable pull as if destiny were pulling my strings." I looked down on Paige, and I didn't have to feign the next part. Not the story nor my admiration for her. "When I first saw my mate, she was facing down six warriors from the Red Wyrm tribe."

Gasps go out around the gathered orcs. Otunga glances sharply at Paige, clearly seeing her in a new light.

"Is this true?" Otunga asks her.

"Well, I was really only …" she clears her throat. "It's true, though I had no illusions about my chances at victory in that fight. If not for Jovak coming along, I would have perished. Or suffered other equally awful fates at their cruel hands."

"It takes more bravery to go into a battle you cannot win instead of the one you know you can." Otunga nods sagely. "Your courage is a testament to your spirit, Paige Holdfast."

"Paige is cunning," I say, smiling as I speak from the heart. "And resourceful, kind, brave, and true. Plus, she knows some medicinal skills. She will bear me wise and mighty children."

Paige stiffens at my side and gives me the

subtlest, quickest narrow-eyed glare I have ever endured. I suppose perhaps that last bit went too far in her estimation.

"But now that I have returned," I say, getting the crowd back on my side, "and have heard of the plight of our people, I am determined to help. I will find the missing orcs and bring them home safely."

"Our Chief!" shouts someone. I can't make them out, but it sounded like it came from my left. I look around, and then someone else shouts.

"Jovak the Noble!"

Now I know that none of my people would say something like that to me. It's just not an orcish turn of phrase. And yet, a shout is carried up, a general chant of praise and commitment to following my leadership and finding the missing tribesmen.

I catch something out of the corner of my eye, a slight motion in the back of the wagon. It's Laney. She ducks back out of sight, and I wonder what she is up to.

"Now, however, the journey has been a long one, and my mate is tired. I must see to her needs and those of her sister who has come into my care."

"Sister?" Otunga glances into the back of the wagon and gasps. "New blood. The chief has brought us new blood."

Paige looks alarmed, but I catch her eye and smile.

"My people believe children to be sacred and the next to bear the banner of our tribe. We are not the same as the Red Wyrm tribe."

She relaxed and nodded.

I led the wagon back to my hut, second in size only to the shaman's temple, which doubles as a hospital and is as much a medical center as a holy place. Once I have both women inside and the door is tightly shut, I turn an awkward look on Paige.

"Thank you," I say. "Your ruse has smoothed things over."

"Don't mention it," Paige replies with a wink.

"Ruse?" Laney grins at both of us. "I might be a kid, but I know that word. Ruse means you guys are just pretending to be mates, right?"

I close my mouth and look at Paige. Paige looks quite uncomfortable. She starts to stammer out a response when Laney talks again.

"Only, you guys aren't really pretending to like each other, are you?" Laney snickers. "You're pretending to like each other and pretending *not* to like each other at the same time."

My face burns with shame because the child has struck the right of things as cleanly as a hammer's head meeting a nail. Laney's gaze darted around the hut, nodding to herself at what she saw.

"Not a bad setup you have here, Chief Jovak. I could get used to it."

She went over to my cold box and opened it.

"Oh, hey, is this smoked salmon?"

Laney took a nibble of the meat and then put it in her mouth.

"Laney …" Paige put her hands on her hips and glared at her younger sibling. "You should ask permission before you touch someone else's food."

"Maybe he should ask permission before he helps himself to my sister."

My eyes and mouth go wide. Paige sputters something unintelligible, and Laney laughs.

"Calm down. I'm just kidding, both of you. It looks like there are two bedrooms. I'll just take this smaller one down the hall."

She moves that way and then turns back to grin at us.

"I'm a very, very deep sleeper. I bet you guys

could make all sorts of noise, and I'd never wake up."

The door closes, and I turn a sheepish expression toward Paige.

"Ah, I'm sorry about her," Paige said with a shrug. "She's very young yet and doesn't understand how things work for grownups."

I can tell by the light in Paige's eyes that she doesn't believe what she says about her sister. I'd say that Laney knows a lot more than her youth would otherwise indicate. She certainly understands the complex dynamic between her big sister and me. Maybe more than I do.

"I greatly appreciate what you are doing for me, Paige," I say slowly. "But perhaps you should have thought it through a bit more?"

"What do you mean by that?" Her eyes clouded over with worry. "Are you angry with me?"

"No!" I cleared my throat and spoke with a bit less vehemence. "That is, no, of course not. I worry about you being uncomfortable. After all, we will now have to keep the ruse going indefinitely."

Paige shrugged and then glanced around my domicile.

"That's okay, I don't mind. I really don't.

Besides, it looks to me like you have plenty of room for both me and Laney."

She's not wrong. I do have more space than I need. The chief's hut is meant to house the chief, his mate, and his family. As I have none of those things, except for pretending, it's room I don't need.

But Laney and her sister need it. I realize now how much it means to me to have helped them both.

"By the way, in the morning, you should thank Laney, too." She stifles a yawn.

"Why?"

"She used her ventriloquism talent earlier to help you out, or didn't you hear?"

"The voices," I say with a gasp. "The voices of the crowd, supporting me. Is she a witch?"

"Not hardly," Paige says with a laugh, her eyes shining. "Ventriloquism is a learned skill. It's throwing your voice, so it sounds like it comes from someplace else."

"A useful ability. I'll be sure to thank her."

"I'm sure she'll get a big kick out of that."

I built a fire in the hearth, and then we ate the smoked salmon and drank cold water from the cistern. Our conversation is mild, and mostly centered on practical matters, but the ease I feel with her makes the whole affair astonishingly pleasant. I feel like it's easier to talk to Paige than anyone I've ever met.

The hour grew late. Paige yawned first, and then I joined in, and soon neither of us could go more than a few sentences without doing so.

"All right," she said, her voice distorted by yet another yawn. "Let's just admit that we're both exhausted and need to sleep soon."

I nod and rise from the rug where we've been sitting.

"You may take my room," I say. "And my bed."

"You want me to take your bed?" She cocks an eyebrow. "And where will you be sleeping?"

Her tone is light and casual, and yet there was an intensity in her gaze when she asked the question. I swallowed the lump in my throat. Why was it suddenly so hot in here? The fire is hardly a raging one. In fact, we've talked so long that it's died to mere embers.

"I can sleep in here on the floor. The bearskin rug is soft enough for an orc's body. It's really no trouble."

Paige rose from her seat, tawny limbs uncrossing as she stood next to me.

"I'll take your bed, Noble Chieftain," she said with mock severity. "But as far as where you're going to sleep, well … that's up to you."

She turned from me and walked toward the door to my bedroom. Was it a trick of the light, or was she shaking her bottom more than necessary?

Paige paused at the door and then gave me a deep, meaningful look … if only I knew which meaning! … and then she went inside, closing the door softly behind her.

I stood there chewing my cud like a fawn-swollen doe, unsure of what to do next. Unsure of even what to think.

If that wasn't an invitation, then I'm a gnome on stilts.

The door closed behind me, and, despite my placid demeanor, my heart was thudding a mile a minute. I can't believe I just said that. I can't believe I just did that! It's scary but also thrilling to think that he might take me up on my offer.

I'm surprised at how spartan it is inside his bedroom. There are no decorations, no banners, and no paintings on the wall. This is a stark contrast from other orc homes I've seen. They usually have keepsakes or trophies from battles, at the very least. His personal space is almost … sterile. Like he's hiding everything about himself rather than splashing it on the walls.

I suppose with him being the Longstrider and

all that, he doesn't spend a whole lot of time in this bedroom. I doubt I'm the first female in here, which kind of makes me jealous for some reason. And yet, I have a feeling that tonight is going to be momentous.

Or so I think until the minutes stretch by, and I start to feel more and more like I've been abandoned. I guess maybe he doesn't want me after all …

The door opens partway. I glanced sharply over and saw Jovak standing there, his eyes burning with hunger. His chiseled chest rises and falls in heavy breaths. I don't know what to do next or what to say.

Don't get me wrong, I know how the love-making thing works on a technical level. It's just that I've never been in this position before. I keep waiting for him to do something, but it's like he's being held back. I don't know if I should encourage him or not.

If I try to embolden him, it might just drive him away instead of bringing him into my web, as it were. But he's just standing there with hungry eyes but immovable feet. I want him to stalk across the floor and take me in those powerful arms of his, and kiss me again.

Slowly, I reached behind my head and gathered the material of my shirt up, never breaking eye contact with him. His eyes widened slightly, his gaze darting down to the expanse of flesh bared on my belly as the shirt lifted from the motion.

My heart is pounding like a drumbeat, and my mind is zinging with excitement. I pulled the shirt off over my head, then tugged it away until my back was bare. Now I am holding the shirt in front of me. It's still on my arms and covering my breasts, but not much else.

At last, I let the shirt slip away and revealed my breasts to him. His pupils dilated, and his nostrils flared as he took in my scent. I'm so ready to go. I'm shaking with need. I've never wanted a man to take me so badly in all my life.

I dropped the shirt to the floor and then grabbed the waist of my mannish trousers. I slid the garment off, down to my knees, and then to my ankles, and then I stepped out of the puddled material.

I now stand naked before him. Jovak moves, at last, entering the room and closing the door behind him. He stalked toward me, and I leaned into him as he took me into his arms. His hands touched my bare back for the first time, and a shiver ran down my spine.

"Paige ..." he breathes my name like a one-word poem, eyes shining and glazed with desire. "Are you certain this is what you want?"

"I've never been more certain of anything." I put my hand on his cheek, caressing the green-gray skin. His eyes squeezed shut as if the touch caused him pain. He trembled, perhaps with fear or many other things roiling inside him. I know the feeling, as I'm in the same boat.

Jovak leaned his face closer to mine. His warm breath tickled my skin, and then I felt the sublime press of his lips upon my own. I accepted his kiss willingly and eagerly. It seems like it's been so long since he last kissed me, though I know it's only been a few days. It might as well have been a decade.

I pressed my body against him, feeling the touch of his skin on mine. His furry loincloth rubbed against my belly, the triangular tip brushing my thighs. His cock twitched under the fur, and the thudding of his heartbeat was so close to my own.

The taste of his mouth is still new to me and yet somehow familiar. It doesn't make any sense, and yet it does. Sort of like the attraction between us. In so many ways, we could not be more different. But right now, we're on the same page. The same frequency. The chemistry is so thick you could scoop it with a fork.

Jovak's kiss grows harder, deeper. His hands crush me to his body. I groan, but not from alarm, fear, or pain. It feels good to have him take me into his arms like this, taking my lips, taking everything, and yet giving back even more.

We came up for air, and our eyes met. He kissed me softly on the lips again, then stepped back to undo the ties on his belt. The loincloth drops to the floor. I take a moment to drink in the sight of him. His body is even more amazing naked, from his broad shoulders to his tapered waist, to the flared bulges of his thighs, which frame the most perfect cock I have ever seen.

His member is standing at attention, ready for me. Jovak took me into his arms again and kissed me. This time nothing is separating us but a sheen of sweat. I moaned into his mouth as he showered me with intense kisses.

Then Jovak dropped his lips to my neck, his hand caressing my hair.

"Paige," he mumbles into my flesh. "I have longed to touch you for an eternity just like this."

I cry out as his words send a deep, primal tremble through my pussy to emanate out to the rest of my body. His touches are like fire, threatening to consume me with passion. I cling to his body as he kisses his way down to my chest.

He carefully kisses each of my nipples before his tongue darts out of his mouth. The first overtly carnal touch, and it's a doozy. My head flew back, and I let out a groan fit to wake the dead. I hope Laney really is as deep a sleeper as she claims.

My nipple hardened under his gentle, teasing ministrations. He suckled on the tender flesh, and I felt a sharp twinge run through my clit. I want him so badly. I want to feel him inside me so much I can't stand it.

The nipple came out of Jovak's mouth with a wet pop. He continued downward, kissing my belly, the soft skin around my navel, and farther down still. Jovak knelt in front of me and pushed my thighs apart with such a sweet dominance that I turned to putty.

His tongue licked slowly through the pink trench between my swollen, wide-open pussy lips. I clutched at his head, bending over and moaning in helpless delight at the sensations he instilled in me.

"Your pussy tastes so good, Paige," he growls into the soft folds of my skin. Then he buried himself in his work, so to speak, and my cry split the air. It feels so incredibly good. Like playing with myself, only much, much better.

His lips envelop my clitoris, and I suck in a ragged gasp of air. Then he suckles, and a silent scream forces its way out of my throat. I took in another deep breath, and this time, my scream made my own ears ring. By god, does he ever know what he's doing down there.

Jovak pushed me back onto the bed, then dove back into his work. His sexy grunts and growls are almost as stimulating as his lips and tongue. I feel the pressure building as a contraction seizes my whole body. Pleasure ripples out in a series of waves that makes me cry out for pleasure. My whole body twists and writhes of its own accord, almost like I'm in agony, only it's anything but painful.

What the hell was that? It must have been an orgasm. I only thought I'd had one before by my own hand. This time there's no doubt. Fuck, I don't know if I can take another one of those, but man, I am eager to try.

Jovak stood to his full height, his cock pointed up. A bead of moisture rolls off the tip and down the shaft until it distends and drips onto my thigh. The feeling of his seed on my body makes me groan with pleasure. I can only imagine what it will be like to feel it inside me.

Jovak grips his veined shaft, his fingers barely able to make it around his member. God, he's huge, but I'm not afraid he'll hurt me. I trust Jovak. He wouldn't let anything bad happen to me.

The head of his throbbing member disappears between my vaginal lips. I gasp as he glides inside me, slowly filling and stretching me ever wider. It feels good, not painful. Jovak is careful not to hurt me, gently gliding in until his cock is in all the way.

I feel a bit of a pinch, almost painful, but it's soon followed by a wave of pleasant sensations when he's finally in fully that are almost as good as the orgasm I just had. Not to mention the orgasm I'm building up to.

Jovak gripped my hips and pulled almost out, and then he thrust into me for the first time. My mouth formed an O as he dragged back out, sending delectable streaks of fire through my entire body. Then he pushed back in, and I cried out sharply.

"Oh god," I cry. "Slower, not so deep."

He obliged, and the next thrust was pure heaven. My eyes squeezed shut as I felt the buildup of another climax coming. On instinct, my body moved with his, my hips raising and grinding as we sought a greater connection and pleasure than ever before.

He feels so good. I almost can't stand it. It's so good I might die. Can you die from pleasure? I think I might if such a thing were possible.

His grunts mingle with the gentle slap of his body against my own. I grit my teeth with a groan as he works me toward my climax. I gripped his chest, my nails raking down his flesh. I can't help myself. I've become a primal beast ruled only by desire. A desire for supreme pleasure exclusively wrought by Jovak's hands alone.

"Oh, Paige," he cries. "Paige, you are so beautiful, so perfect!"

His words are like champagne raining on my brain. I feel an excited rush of pleasure spread through my nerve endings like wildfire.

He cried out, coming inside me. Then I find out a secret about the orc cock ... it vibrates like mad after expelling its seed. As I writhe beneath his powerful body, my ragged breath predates a sharp, desperate cry of pleasure.

He collapsed on top of me, kissing me gently as our sweat mingled and cooled. I wrapped all four limbs around him as if I intended to never let him go.

Maybe it's just pretending. Maybe we're not really mates. And yet, for this night, it seems very real.

12

JOVAK

The first morning after I brought Paige back as my mate, I stepped out of my hut and prepared myself for the usual stares filled with barely contained contempt. I happened to match gazes with an orcish messenger bustling down the paved road of our settlement.

He gave me a nod, his eyes filled with cautious neutrality. It's not adoration, but it's a far cry from what I'm used to. Is this because they think I've taken a mate? Curious to see if the effect has spread beyond this one individual, I take a tour of the city. I'm not just indulging my curiosity or my ego. I also intend to ask about the missing tribesmen. It's unlikely, but perhaps I can uncover something that links the disappearances on our end.

I make my way past the stalls where the humans have their surplus foodstuffs for sale. One of the sellers smiles at me and hands me a canvas rucksack bulging with apples.

"What's this for?" I ask.

"For your new mate and her little sister. And for you, of course, my chief."

He bows his wizened head, and I sigh.

"For the last time, Nails, one does not bow to chieftains. I am not some arrogant dark elf king who thinks everyone should be bowing and scraping all the time. The chief is the first servant of the people."

He nodded like he always does.

"Of course, Chief Jovak. Sorry to offend you."

"You have not offended me, Nails. Thank you for the apples."

I continue through the town, and the response is the same. The orcs are a bit subtler in their demeanors than the humans, but the fact remains that they are all treating me differently.

The day was hot, and I stopped in the shade of a birch tree, leaning my back against the rough bark. I use a rag to mop sweat from my forehead when I hear two orcs talking on the other side of the tree.

"You think the chief will not wander any longer now that he's taken a mate?"

"I wouldn't think so," replies the other, who sounds a bit older. "His mate will not stand for him being out and about all the time. This could be a sign that our chieftain has matured at last."

A wry grin crosses my face. I had not expected the effect to go quite this far. I suppose it does represent a massive lifestyle change for me to have taken a mate.

Only, the mating is not for real. Well, the mating act certainly was. I feel warmth spreading through my body just thinking of the night I'd spent with Paige.

But our being mates is only a ruse. Only Laney knows the truth, so far. I fear that it will make my people angrier if they should find out the truth.

I stop by a small orc home on the outskirts of the city and rap on the door. A moment later, the timbers creak, and I'm faced with the careworn features of a middle-aged human woman. She seems startled to see me.

"Chief Jovak? What are you doing here?"

"I have come to ask you a few questions about Moldar, your missing mate."

Her face clouds over with worry.

"He's been gone for over a week, vanished without a trace. I don't know what I can tell you that I haven't already told Rolar and the others."

"I know this is hard for you, Amy, but please, indulge me. It could be that you might remember some small detail that you neglected to mention before."

She nods and steps back, allowing me passage to her humble home. I see a great stuffed chair by the fireplace. Its worn areas suggest Moldar liked to sit there in particular. Their children have long since reached adulthood and moved out into their own houses, making the home seem rather empty. I feel she must be terribly lonely.

"Would you like some tea?" she asks.

"Just water would be fine." I can't imagine drinking a hot beverage after having been out in the sun for so long.

She brought me the water along with a plate of sliced tomatoes and a fat wedge of goat cheese. It would be rude not to take at least a small bite, but the cheese and tomato are surprisingly great together. I refrain from taking another bite and instead fix her with my gaze.

"Amy, did Moldar say anything about where he was going that day he vanished?"

"No," she said, shaking her head. "I think he was supposed to patrol the western forest. That's what Rolar said anyway."

I nod. Rolar is likely right about that.

"And was he acting strangely? Any disruptions in his sleep or odd behavior?"

"No," she says, shaking her head vehemently. "He was just like he always was. A little bit grumpy, but he always meant well. Now he's gone, and I'm all alone …."

She covers her face with her hands. I stood and put my hand on her shoulder.

"I will do everything I can to get him back, I swear."

She nodded and wiped her tears. I found out precious little from her or any of the others I interviewed. All of the loved ones of the missing warriors say the same thing … nothing stood out as strange before they disappeared.

That rules out depression, madness, or discontent with their lot. Also, any kind of conspiracy where the missing warriors were planning a coup. That had been one of my concerns.

Unfortunately, the more I investigate, the more certain I am that something sinister has happened to our missing brethren.

I coordinated efforts with my warriors and sent out a dozen search parties. I even drew back from our border defense, though I am loath to do so. It might leave us open to an enemy scout or even an attack, but if we don't find out what happened to those missing warriors soon, I fear that there could be trouble.

I head back to my home, and when I open the door, my jaw drops open.

"What did you do to my house?" I sputter.

Laney stops with a broom in one hand and a dustpan in the other. "We cleaned it," she says cleverly with a note of recrimination in her young voice.

"And organized some things," Paige says, coming out of the bedroom with a stack of worn clothing in her arms. "I hope you don't mind, but we wanted to do something useful for you since you took us into your home."

I look around my hut. Nothing is where I left it

before. How am I supposed to find anything now? Yes, it was a little bit dusty in here, but it wasn't that bad … was it?

I looked into Paige's crystalline eyes and realized that I could not be angry with her.

"No, this is good. I'm glad for the help. I suppose I've rather neglected things around here for some time."

Paige relaxed, and a smile blossomed on her face. That smile makes my heart leap for joy. Why am I having all of these feelings? It's troublesome. That's what it is. Now I have a house where I can't find anything and, and …

And a woman I believe I have come to care for very much.

"Where have you been all day?" Laney asks.

I gave her a look. "I could ask you the same question. You should have been at school."

"School?" Laney blinks. "What's that?"

"Grandpa told me about it. Before the portals opened, kids your age went to a special building where they learned all sorts of things." Paige puts a hand on Laney's shoulder. "I think it's a great idea for you to go, Laney. You'll make lots of friends."

"Okay," Laney shrugged and went back to cleaning. "But Jovak never answered my question."

"Indeed, I did not. I was out speaking to the families of those who are missing. Not to mention trying to organize more search parties, though we are spread thin already."

"Did you find out anything?" Paige asks.

I shook my head sadly, and then we prepared a meal. My life is nearly perfect for the next few days, except for the missing orcs. Laney spends all day at the school, which gives Paige and me plenty of alone time. I make love to her at least once a day, if not more. She performs all the functions of a mate, including taking care of the household, while I perform my duties as chieftain.

Neither of us ever mention the big shadow hanging over our heads. Namely, that this is a fake relationship. A staged play performed for the entirety of our tribe, who have no idea they're watching a production.

While Paige and I lay together in each other's arms, our sweat mingling as it cools, I tell her the news I've been keeping from her.

"I will be joining the search parties soon."

"You will? But why? No disrespect …" She props herself up on my chest, her cheek resting on my breast. "But what difference is one more orc going to make?"

"I'm not just any orc. I am the Longstrider. No one has traveled these lands more than I have. I know places, dens, valleys, and caverns that might be fruitful in the search. Plus, it will make me feel as if I'm actually doing something to help rather than just waiting for news along with everyone else."

"Well, just be careful. I don't want you to go missing too."

I almost scoff at what she says until I realize how worried she is. I kiss her instead. "I will be careful. I have no intention of joining the ranks of those missing."

I made love to her again, and it occurred to me that the lines between fakery and reality were starting to blur.

Later, when Laney was to return from school soon, I helped her carry a big pot of water to the wood-burning stove for our dinner porridge.

A shout from outside gave us both pause. I rushed outside and found one of the search parties. Then I noticed a body lying prone on a litter between them and ran over to join them.

"What happened?" I ask.

"We found Moldar," says Rolar, his jaw set hard. "He lives, but …"

His voice trails off, and I peer down on what we call a litter. I assume Paige would call it a bed on wheels. My mouth flew open in shock at what I beheld.

"By the ancestors, what sorcery is this?"

13

PAIGE

I work my way through the milling throng surrounding the injured tribesman. At least, I think he's injured. I heard someone in the crowd say that he was still alive, but that might not be true.

"What's going on?" Laney asks.

I turn around, shocked to see her standing there. "Laney, you need to go back to the house now."

She frowned, her little face scrunched up with petulance. "But I want to see what's going on."

"You're too little. You're going to get knocked over in this crowd and trampled to death. Just go."

"But there are kids here younger than me," she protests.

She's not wrong, but I can't let her win this argument. I won't feel right until I know she's safe. Besides, the tribesman is likely badly injured even if he is alive. I don't want her to get scared looking at him.

"Laney," I say, my voice on the verge of breaking. "Please mind me. I just can't concentrate on anything else until I know you're safe. Please."

Laney rolled her eyes and heaved an exasperated sigh. "Fine, but you'd better tell me everything that happened when you get back. I know you think I'm just a little kid, but I've already seen dead bodies before. Lots of them."

She turned and jogged back to our … that is, to Jovak's house. I return to my efforts to shoulder my way to the front of the crowd.

When I finally succeeded, I almost wished I hadn't. The warriors bearing the bed on wheels continued on their way toward the shaman's temple. Already I can hear Shaman Otunga's scratchy voice demanding to see the patient.

But my eyes are transfixed on the tribesman or what's left of him. He looks diminished, skin loose and pruned as if he's been sucked dry by a horde of mosquitoes. I can see several raw, open wounds. My hand claps over my mouth at how ghastly and large the wounds are. I could have put my entire hand into one of them if I was inclined to try.

Yet, the wounds do not bleed. I'm not sure he has any blood left. Somehow, his chest continues to rise and fall with his respiration. His eyes are closed, and his mouth is open. He has something dark stuck to several of his teeth, like he's been eating dirt.

"Enough!"

Otunga's voice carries the weight of authority and a little boost of magic. A gust of wind blows hard down the paved road, and the orcs and humans part for her. She clacks up on her walking stick, moving faster than I would have thought possible for one at her advanced age.

She puts a gnarled hand on the tribesman's forehead and closes her eyes. Her lips move with the words of a spell. Then she opens her eyes and turns her gaze on Rolar.

"Get him into the temple, quickly. He is near death."

I join the procession as they head into the temple. Most of the orcs and humans are told to wait outside. I think I'm only allowed in because I'm Jovak's mate.

They put the tribesman onto a padded table. He

looks so frail, so unlike all of the orcs I've seen, even the old ones. So withered, a mere husk of what he should be. Jovak catches my gaze and frowns.

"Perhaps you should wait outside," he says.

"I'm no stranger to tragedy, Jovak. I'll stay unless you command me to leave."

He seemed taken aback, then subtly nodded.

"What's wrong with him?" he asks Otunga.

She scowled as she passed her hands over the man's body.

"He is like the prey of a spider trapped in a silken cocoon. Much of his body has been dissolved away. I think he's been fed upon."

"Fed upon?" Jovak's alarm mirrors my own. My heart skips a beat at the thought of something powerful and evil enough to feed on orc warriors. "By what? What manner of creature would do this?"

Jovak turns to Rolar.

"Where did you find him?"

"In the western forest," Rolar replied grimly. "We were searching, and then his body just … sort of rose from the dirt."

"You mean he dug his way out of a shallow grave," Jovak says.

"No, my chief." I can't help but notice Rolar is far more respectful than he was upon our first meeting. "I mean that he came up out of the dirt. He was in no shape to dig himself out. It was as if … the forest was expunging him like so much waste."

"Sorcery," Otunga spits and makes a sign in the air to ward off evil. "Dark elves do not care if they pollute the land itself."

"You mean to say the forest is taking our people?" Jovak frowns. "That makes no sense."

"What does when the damnable pointy ears are involved?" Rolar says. For some reason, he gives Jovak a very sharp look … an expression Jovak noticed but chose not to react to. There's a story there, but of course, there's no time to get into it now. It wouldn't be appropriate anyway.

"We should concentrate our search parties on the western forest," Jovak says. "And make sure no band is smaller than ten orcs."

"What good is an entire army of orcs if the forest itself has turned against us?" Rolar asks.

"Perhaps not much," Jovak admits. "But the more orcs in the search party, the more chance that at least one of them will be able to escape this evil and report back to us."

Rolar's eyes narrow to slits.

"So you would sacrifice nine orcs just to satisfy your curiosity?"

Jovak rears up to his full height.

"No, you fool. I would sacrifice a hundred orcs to find out why our people are vanishing and put a stop to it. Including myself. I will join the search personally."

I flinched because I was hoping Jovak had abandoned that idea when he saw the condition his tribesman was in.

Right about then, a woman shoved her way in the door, leaving two befuddled guards in her wake. The orcs could easily have stopped this aging human woman, but they let her through. I found out why a moment later. She threw herself at the lean figure on the table.

"Moldar," she cries. "My Moldar, what has happened to you?"

"Do not touch him," Otunga says. "He is very frail, and the lightest shock could kill him."

"Moldar's mate," Jovak whispered in my ear. "Amy. She is one of those I interviewed."

I nodded, feeling very sorry for her.

Jovak turned to Otunga.

"Can you do anything for Moldar?"

She made a low hum in the back of her throat like she was considering things.

"I can give him a fighting chance. Our magic is returning but is still much weaker than it was on Protheka. I cannot replace what was lost, but his body should be able to regrow it, given time and proper care. He must be fed a thin broth or gruel several times a day and given fluids more often than that."

"What about his wounds?"

She examined the holes, poking her fingers inside in a way that made me sick to my stomach.

"There is no sign of infection … wait, is this pus?"

She pulled her finger out and gaped at the clear yellow-brown ichor on the tip. She sniffs and frowns.

"It smells like tree sap."

"He has tree sap in his wounds? But how?" Jovak asks.

"I do not know. But the sap, I suspect, has a wound-cleaning property. Otherwise, I would expect a bad infection to set in, given the size of these wounds."

Jovak turned to Rolar.

"I need you to put the word out to everyone in

the tribe, humans and orcs alike. Until this crisis is over, *no one* is to go out alone. Everyone should travel in bands of at least two. Three or more would be preferable."

"As you will, my Chief." Rolar bounces out of the temple and starts bellowing. He gathers some of his warriors together and sets them to the task of spreading the chief's edict.

There doesn't seem to be much of anything we can do for poor Moldar right now, so Jovak and I take our leave and let the shamans do their work. The last thing I hear before the door closes is Otunga asking for a human physician to come and check on Moldar as well.

We walked back to his house in relative silence. That night, we made love in a desperate yet soothing way. Neither of us talked about how much danger Jovak was going to be walking into if he joined the search.

I managed to hold my tongue until the very morning of the day he was due to leave. Jovak isn't dressed for travel in a simple loincloth and boots. He's dressed for battle. An iron breastplate with mail sleeves and a chain mail skirt that reaches his knees don't seem like they'll be much protection against something that can suck a full-grown orc dry.

When I gave voice to my worries, Jovak stopped on the doorstep and turned to face me.

"Paige, I promise to be careful."

"I know, but you think Moldar wasn't careful? Or any of the others?"

He grew tight-lipped, but then I saw something burning in his eyes. Jovak suddenly takes me by the arms and holds me close to him.

"Paige …" his voice is a velvet whisper, this tone thick with meaning. "Ever since I met you, my heart has ached. I feel as if you are the one, the one I've been waiting to meet my whole life."

My mouth gapes open. Is he telling me that he's falling in love with me? Or that he has already? I don't know what to say.

I feel guilt more than anything. I feel like I should have stronger feelings for Jovak, but I'm just not sure about it yet. So much has happened so fast. I do like him, and maybe I am really starting to care for him …

Or maybe it's just gratitude because he helped Laney and me so much.

Whatever the case, he took my silence as a

rejection. His eyes grew bitter and hard, and he turned his broad back on me.

"Jovak," I cried as he strode away from me. "Wait, please. Don't just go and leave things like this …."

But he's already gone. I closed the door and turned my back, resting against it. I feel like I want to collapse. It's all so much, too much, roiling around in my belly and in my head. I want to scream, and I want to throw up, and most of all, I want to run after Jovak and tell him … what? I don't know. I just don't know.

I look up and see Laney standing there, watching me with knowing eyes.

"Why did you let him go like that?"

"How am I supposed to stop him, Laney?"

She looks at me hard for a long moment, then speaks.

"Paige, do you love him?"

Silence is the only answer I can give.

14

JOVAK

I was a fool to think that Paige's heart actually beat for me.

It is a fake relationship, after all. She's not really my mate. She's my mate in name only. How could I have been so stupid?

And now I have perhaps ruined any chance of us being together by moving things too far, too fast. I only wanted to be happy with Paige, but … perhaps I do want more. I want what we have to be real and not just a fantasy.

I have to put her from my mind … impossible! … but I must try. Or at least move her to the back of my thoughts. Now is not the time for heartbreak or despondency. Now is the time for action.

I head into the city square, where I have told

my search party to gather. They perk up at my approach. A dozen orc warriors, most of them blooded in battle, all of them eager to find their missing brethren.

My tracker, a one-eyed orc named Vaerlik, stands from the low wall surrounding the public fountain and picks up his longbow. He nods to me and then gestures at his fellows.

"We are ready to follow you, Chief Jovak."

"I never had any doubts as to your readiness, Vaerlik. I know that you have spent long, tireless hours out in the forest searching. No doubt you are disillusioned, and the prospect of returning is a daunting one, but I must call on you to serve our people again."

"Do not worry for me, Chief." His eyes narrow to slits. "Moldar has been found, so that means there is hope the rest of our folk are alive as well. And it is a point of pride to me that I return to the search. Until I have turned over every leaf, looked behind every tree trunk and branch, I will not stop until our people are recovered."

"Good lad," I say, clapping him on the shoulder. I turn to address the rest of the search party. "I have news for all of you. This morning, Moldar awakened and spoke."

A sharp cheer goes up as my fellows thrust their weapons in the air with joy.

"Moldar has a warning for us," I say, my tone growing low and growly. "He is yet weak and cannot remain awake for long. But he grabbed my arm with his returning strength and told me, 'beware the brambles.'"

"Beware the brambles?" Vaerlik growls. "What brambles? There are brambles all over the forest."

"Then we'd best beware of everything, hadn't we?" I turn my gaze on all of them in turn. "I am not commanding anyone to join me on this search and recovery mission. Our way will be perilous, and I have no idea what dangers we might face, only that we will face them. If any of you wish to turn back, now is the time."

No one makes a move, and the aura grows awkward and uncomfortable.

"I am serious." My eyes narrow. "I am not trying to call out any of you for being cowards. If anyone wants to walk away and remain behind with their families, I will not judge you as a coward. I will only judge you as being far more intelligent than the rest of us."

I smile a bit at the end, and a ragged laugh goes up. Still, not one orc chooses to abandon the search. Vaerlik grabs my arm and tugs me a short distance away, speaking softly so only I can hear him.

"My Chief, I do not think we should take Kotar with us."

"Why not? Is he a poor warrior, a bad tracker?"

"No, he is a fine warrior and an … adequate tracker." Vaerlik shook his head as if to clear it. "However, his human mate has just found out from the shaman Otunga that she is with child."

I nod, then turn to the warrior in question.

"Kotar," I say. "You will remain behind. I think eleven warriors is enough for this search party, and you have duties here."

"But, my Chief," Kotar says, exasperated. "I am ready to do my part to find our lost kin."

"I know you are. No one doubts your courage or your commitment. But this could be dangerous, and you have a child on the way."

Kotar sighed, hanging his head. "As you will, my Chief."

"Don't be upset, Kotar. You have a growing family."

"Do you not also have a family, my Chief?"

I flinch as if I've been struck because his question reminds me of the bad parting I just had with Paige.

"Never mind that," I snarl. "My mate is not with child, and I have a duty to the tribe. I have been away too much and for too long. I must atone."

No one argues with me, and I set off toward the edge of town with my band of searchers. Without Kotar, of course. Once we leave the safety of the city behind, the forest envelops us in its verdant embrace.

"Is it just me," Vaerlik says in a low voice, "or is the forest more sinister than usual?"

"I think it's just you," I reply. "We are still many miles from where Moldar was found."

"It doesn't hurt to be wary anyway, my Chief."

I laugh and slap him on his back. "No, it does not hurt at all."

We spread out into a line. Better to move through the narrow game trails. Every so often, I ask them to sound off. One by one, they call their names aloud and reassure me they are still with us.

The journey takes us into the denser woods. Our game trail grows narrower until I can barely make it out. The sun struggles to shine through the thick boughs overhead. Only a small amount of light reaches the forest floor.

Our journey is silent except for when the others call out their names. We continue on the path and come across numerous brambles. Yet none of them seem all that sinister.

Then we march single file up a steep hill, and I feel like something is off. I can't describe the feeling other than it seems like something terrible is breathing down my neck. The others sense it, too, glancing about sharply in the near darkness and gripping their weapons all the more tightly.

"We're nearly to the place where they found him," Vaerlik says from the front of our band.

"Then we'd best look sharp," I snap. "Let's make sure everyone is still with us. Roll call!"

One by one, the orcs in our band call out their names. All save one.

"Burr?" I frown and look to the rear of the line. "Burr, can you hear us?"

The band stopped, and everyone exchanged nervous glances.

"He was right behind me a moment ago," says one of the orcs. "He can't have gone far."

We moved back the way we came, calling out Burr's name. I worry that someone else will disappear.

"Staggered whistling," I call out.

I start the whistle, and when I die down, another warrior takes it up. This way, we can constantly keep track of each other in the woods. The trunks force us to break up our line, and that concerns me. Then the inevitable happens.

One of the orcs fails to whistle back.

"Everyone freeze," I cry. "Don't move. Back to the game trail, now."

"But now there are two of us missing," cries one of the search party.

"And I don't want anyone else to get lost. Vaerlik, you agree with me, right?"

Silence.

"Vaerlik?"

I shout his name louder, and then his scream splits the air. I ran in the direction it came from. The sounds of other orcs crashing through the underbrush mean I'm not alone. At least, not for now. Yet it seems like there should be more, far more.

I charge through the forest, unmindful of thorns and brambles tearing at my clothing and skin. It almost seems as if the forest itself is trying to prevent me from getting to Vaerlik. The tracker's scream comes again, and I run even faster.

I burst through the tree line into a clearing. My

eyes widen as I stare at a tree with a gnarled, grotesquely shaped trunk. Its bark is so dark red as to be almost black, and not a single leaf remains on its dead branches. The tree must be twice as big around as the next largest I've seen in this forest.

But it's what's pinned to the tree that really captures my attention. Or rather, who. Vaerlik hangs from the trunk about twenty feet in the air. Vines encircle his limbs and throat, choking off his next scream.

Right before my eyes, the vines burrow into his shoulders, sneaking in past the gaps in his armor. Vaerlik cries out in agony despite the tight hold on his throat. Now I know what caused Moldar's wounds.

My axes are in my hands. I don't even recall drawing them. I charge the tree, intending to climb up and free him.

A sharp cry from my left stops me cold. I turn just in time to see another orc being dragged away into the underbrush by more of the red vines. Suddenly the clearing is alive with them, whipping about and hissing through the air, almost like snakes.

A thick one entangles around my leg. I shouted and brought my ax down on it, severing it in two.

The halves fall apart and spurt thick sap all around, the same sap I saw at the shaman's temple back at Shattered Rock.

I hacked at more vines that were trying to entangle me. I have to get to the tracker, but I don't see how it's possible. I can't even see him for all of the vines assaulting me. With horror, I realize that if I remain another moment, I'll be imprisoned too.

My first thought is that I have to get back to Paige, no matter what. I do something that makes me feel about as low as a snake.

I flee.

I raced out of the clearing. The vines were tearing at me and trying to hold me back. I missed a step and tumbled down a steep hill, falling head over heels. At least the vines plague me no longer as they seem to stop at the top of the hill.

I tried to stop my mad descent, but I've got too much momentum. Then I'm not rolling. I'm just falling, nothing beneath me but air. I hit the ground hard and tumbled into a stone-walled pit. I only had a moment to react before I slammed into the bottom. My vision grows dark at the edges. I look up and see a little circle of light at the top. An old human well. At least the vines can't get me here.

But the walls are too far apart to climb, too steep with no handholds. I will not be getting out of here on my own power. How will anyone even know I am down here or how to find me? Have I come so far only to die in so ignoble a fashion?

My only thought is that I will never see Paige again. The despair was far worse than the pain of my injuries as I huddled up on the floor of the well.

It may not be hopeless, but it's close enough to count.

15

PAIGE

I hefted my pack onto my back and gave Amy a thankful smile.

"I really appreciate you looking after Laney while I'm gone."

Amy returned my smile, though a bit weakly. Her mate, Moldar, is still touch and go. He's recovering from his ordeal, but the shaman Otunga refuses to say he's out of the woods yet.

"It's really no trouble. The house feels rather empty. It will be good to have the sound of a child's laughter again."

I smile, but I'm not sure how much laughing Laney is going to do. She's still pretty upset with me for not taking her with me into the forest. I intend to find Jovak. He's been gone for over a day, along with the entirety of his search party.

Laney snorted derisively and gave me a dirty look.

"Why are you even going to look for him? Half the tribe is searching for Jovak."

"I know, Laney."

"How are you going to find him without me? You've always had me to look out for you, big sis. Without me, you're going to fall down a hole or something."

"I'll be careful, Laney, but this is no game. He could be hurt, or even …" My voice breaks and my eyes get misty. Amy puts her hand on my shoulder.

"I know how you feel, Paige. But my mate came back to me. That means there's a good chance your mate is still alive."

My *pretend* mate, she means. I feel a stab of guilt about that, given what Jovak was trying to tell me before he left. He just took me by surprise, is all. How am I supposed to know how I feel when he's the first man I've ever really been involved with? Is this going to last forever? There are too many unknowns. I've been let down by too many people to just let myself trust him now.

Laney hugged me tight, burying her face in my

stomach, all of her bravado flown for the time being.

"Be careful. You're all I have, you know," Laney said as moisture built in her eyes.

"That's not true. You have friends at school. Not to mention an entire tribe of orcs who essentially see you as a princess." I wasn't sure my fake joy seeped through to Laney.

"Do they really?" She looked up at me with a start.

"Of course, they do. You're the, ah, sister-in-law of the chief, aren't you? That makes you kind of like royalty." I try to hide the smirk starting to build.

"I think you're just trying to make me feel better."

"Is it working?" I should have realized that Laney reads me so well that she could tear off the mask and see what is lurking in my mind and heart.

She gave me a crooked half-smile and shrugged.

"It's not *not* working. Be safe. If you don't come back soon, I'm going to sneak out and find you."

That's plenty of motivation for me to return, even more than the fact that I don't particularly want to die. I take my leave of them and head for the forest. The settlement is almost empty, with so many searching for the missing orcs.

Not to mention the missing chief.

It makes it easy to sneak off. I'm not sure if they would try to stop me or not, being the chief's *mate*, but I don't want to take the chance.

It's probably stupid of me to think I can do something that the orc search parties can't. Maybe Laney is right, and I'm wasting my time.

But if there's even a chance I can find him or help to find him, then I have to take it. Besides, I'm going crazy sitting around waiting for him to come back. I shouldn't have let him leave on such a sour note. I should have told him I'm not rejecting him. I'm just not sure how I feel yet.

I can't stand the thought of him dying. I can stand the thought of him dying while thinking I don't care for him at all, even less.

I set off on one of the game trails that crisscross the forest. I spot a big orcish boot print in the mud right away, so I know I'm on the right trail. Of course, there are already orcs searching, so it might be one of them. But Jovak has a particularly wide stride, and the boot prints are spread out far enough that I think it has to be the Longstrider.

I rush along the trail for a while, stumbling from time to time as the leaves overhead grow so dense the sunlight barely makes it down here. I can hardly see my hand in front of my face.

I have to keep going, for Jovak's sake, as much as my own. I've been wandering around this land for quite some time too. I might not be the Longstrider, but I know my way around the woods.

The only weapon I brought with me is an orcish short sword. Yeah, short for an orc. For me, it's a full-sized blade. I asked Jovak to show me how to use a sword. He taught me a few very basic moves, but I have no illusions about how long I'll last in an actual fight.

But I get the feeling that what's out here taking orcs isn't something you can best with a sword anyway. Sorcery, the shamans said. I'm not equipped to deal with sorcery, but from what I understand, magic is weak on this side of the portal. Maybe there's something I can do to help.

I march through the woods for hours, finding the occasional sign that the orcish search party has been through ahead of me. I find the boot prints, snapped twigs, broken brambles, and other trailblazing marks that give my heart hope I'm on the right track.

Then I find a place along the trail marked by numerous broken branches, trampled leaves, and boot prints all headed the same way. My heart thuds hard in my chest. This is it. This is where they left the road.

I start to follow, and then I hear something ... a sharp, shrill whistle that cuts through the heavy, humid forest air. No way was that sound made by an animal. An orcish signal, perhaps? There are many searchers in the woods. If I follow the sound of the whistle, I might not ever make my way back to this spot. The woods are that dense.

And yet, I get a strange feeling in my chest. For some reason, I don't think I should follow the trail. I feel like I should follow that whistle instead.

I hem and haw for a bit and then ultimately decide to follow the whistle. Fortunately, it repeats every so often. I pick my way up the trail and then find myself standing at the top of a very steep hill.

My eyes widen when I see the signs that someone has tumbled down here recently. There are deep indents in the grass where orcish armor has gouged the terrain. I spot an orc-made water-skin hooked on an upturned root.

My heart skips a beat when I realize I know this waterskin. The red sun design on the flat part of the bottle gives it away. I remember Jovak telling me that the skin was a gift from their friends in the Crimson Sun tribe.

That's Jovak's waterskin, or I'm an orc with a pituitary condition.

Carefully, I pick my way down the steep slope. I don't want to go falling down it, too, and wind up getting hurt. The whistle comes again, splitting the air from much closer now. I toy with the idea of whistling back, but for all I know, that would be a bad idea. It might confuse whatever orc is trying to send a signal.

Also, it would pinpoint my location in the woods. I don't know if maybe whoever took the missing orcs is behind the whistle. It's best if I remain silent for the time being and try to locate the source as quickly as possible.

I made it to the waterskin and picked it up, putting the thong over my shoulder. I hope I get the chance to give it back to Jovak. Maybe he's the one who's been whistling? Again I'm tempted to try to whistle myself, but caution rules it out.

Finally, I make it to a less steep portion of the hill, and not a moment too soon. I stop myself just before I reach the sudden drop-off. A sheer drop of at least fifteen feet precedes a wide, flat expanse. It looks like there used to be a homestead here or maybe a farm of some kind.

I skirt around the cliff until I find a less extreme, if much slower, path to the homestead. As I reach the flat terrain, the whistle comes again. I pinpointed the source as coming from the farthest end from where I stand.

Carefully, I picked my way across, my eyes on alert for danger. I draw the sword at my side and hold it awkwardly in front of me. I follow the signs of passage when the whistle comes again, so sharp that it hurts my ears.

I looked down and gasped. Another step, and I'd have fallen right into a deep, wide hole. No, not a hole. An old well, judging by the masonry on the sides. Someone built this with a great deal of effort, and probably the construction equipment that humans lost during the invasion.

I peer down into the well and can just see something moving at the bottom.

"Hello, down there," I call out.

"Paige?"

My lips spread into a wide smile at the sound of Jovak's voice.

"Yeah, it's me," I call down. "Are you all right?"

"I am not hurt badly, but I cannot climb out of this pit either."

"Okay, it's all right. Let me see if I can find a rope or something."

I searched the ruined barn at the edge of the clearing. This is not an easy task, as one of the walls has collapsed inward and covered most of the interior. Fortunately, it breaks apart with ease due to heavy rot.

Later, after a lot of splinters and cursing, I finally locate what I seek. A long, algae-covered length of rope. The algae makes it smell bad, but when I give it a few experimental tugs, the rope holds together just fine.

It will have to do. I dragged the surprisingly heavy bundle over to the well. I'm wearing a glistening sheen of sweat by the time I finally make it.

"Hang on, Jovak," I call. "I found a rope. I'm going to secure it around this old tree stump and throw you the other end."

I only hope it's long enough. I tied the rope around the trunk and then tossed the end down the hole.

"Ow!" Jovak said as it whapped him in the face.

I guess it's long enough.

He gripped the rope and climbed up, hand over hand, grunting with the effort. My heart leapt with joy when he hauled his green-skinned body out of the hole and dragged himself to his feet.

"Jovak," I cry, going to him. He holds me tightly, his big hand petting my hair in the way that I like.

"Oh, Paige," he whispers. "I thought I'd lost you."

"Never," I say, holding him tighter and pressing my face into his chest so he can't see my tears.

The feeling of having Paige back in my arms is sublime. There are many conflicting emotions flowing through me, not the least of which is some measure of resentment at how we parted last.

Only I feel like that doesn't matter any longer. What does matter is that she came for me. She saved my life, in fact. If not for her happening along, I may not ever have gotten out of that hole.

I pulled away from her and put my hand on her soft cheek. Her eyes closed slightly, then opened again.

"Jovak, what happened? How did you end up in the well?"

"I fell down a steep hill, and my momentum was not stopped in time."

She rolls her eyes.

"Obviously, yes, but what happened before that? Where is the rest of your search party? Weren't you bragging about how you were going to bring along the best tracker in your tribe or something like that?"

My jaw was set hard, and my voice came out as a growl.

"I did bring the best tracker. I brought along some of the finest warriors at my disposal as well. It was all for naught because our foe is not one that can be felled with a sword or ax. Well, perhaps by ax, but I don't know how we would ever get close enough without being captured ourselves."

Paige looks kind of annoyed.

"Look, I just got here, okay? How about you try being a little less vague? What did you find? What's been kidnapping the tribesmen?"

"As strange as it may sound, I think it was a tree."

Paige looks at me for a long time as if she's waiting to see if I'm making a jest.

"Wait, you're not kidding, are you?" she asks.

"You really think it's a tree that's doing this to your people?"

"I don't have to think. I know." I sigh. "It's not a normal tree. I suspect it has been twisted by dark elf magic or perhaps orcish magic. I am not a shaman. I do know that the tree has lost all of its leaves. Leaves are like a tree's mouth. It's how they gobble up sunlight. Without leaves, the tree should have starved, only …"

It takes me a moment to put the rest of it together. "Only the tree found an alternative source of nutrition. Namely sticking its roots into living creatures and sucking them dry."

"So that's what happened to Moldar?" Paige looks worried. "But if that's true, then why did the tree let him go?"

"I have been wondering that myself. I have a theory."

"Oh?" She arches her brows. "Let's hear this."

"I believe the magic not only crippled the tree's leaves, but it also gave it the ability to move. And things that move, often, are things that think, even if it's only in a crude way. I think that the tree let Moldar go as a means to lure more victims to its fell grove."

"You think it's that smart?"

"With magic, anything is possible. It possesses a low cunning, at the least. Not only did it use Moldar to lure more of us to it, but it also used my tracker to draw the rest of the search party into its clutches."

"Well, if it took out your entire party, what chance do you and I have?" Paige shakes her head. "I want to help, but maybe … I hate to say it, but maybe we should just keep away from this area of the forest. Let the tree have it and move on."

I give this some thought. Actually, when I was down in the well, I had much the same idea. But one thing stopped me, as it does now, from carrying it out.

"The tree has not killed its victims, at least not all of them," I say slowly. "That means there's still a chance we can save them. And if not, well … perhaps using bow and arrow, we could give them a cleaner kind of death with less suffering."

Paige shudders.

"I hope it doesn't come to that. Oh, Jovak, there must be something we can do! Maybe if we build a fire near the tree's roots?"

"Maybe, but we would likely kill our own people in an effort to destroy the tree."

Her eyes cloud over. At first, I think she's

wallowing in despair, but then I see the light of cunning in her gaze.

"You have an idea?" I ask.

"Maybe. It depends on if what I found in that rusted drum is what I think it is."

She leads me to the ruins of the old barn. The wood is so rotten it comes apart at the lightest touch. I'm a little worried the rest of the structure will fall in on us, and I keep a watchful eye on it.

"Here it is." She brushes away some vines from a metal barrel covered with a red sheen of rust. Paige looks around in the ruins, then draws her sword. She jams the tip into a recession running around in a circle on top of the barrel.

"What are you doing?" I ask, aghast. "That will ruin the point of your blade."

"Maybe, but it's not much good against a monster tree anyway. What's inside of here might be."

She rubs vigorously on the side of the barrel. Rust rains down, dusting the grass below with scarlet. Some words in the old human tongue are scrawled across the surface.

"You know what this says?" she asks.

"No, I do not read the human tongue."

"It says *Roundup*. It's a vegetation killer left over

from before the fall of humanity. If the contents are still good, we can use it against the tree."

"And how will we get this Roundup to the tree without being captured ourselves?"

"Hmm." Her brows come together, knitting in thought. "I might have an idea about that. Tell me, does the tree only eat orcs, or will it eat anything?"

I frown and try to remember the brief flashes I can recall of my near capture.

"I do not know … wait!" My mouth opens with a gasp. "Yes, I do think I saw something else in the tree. Something with antlers … a deer, perhaps."

"Okay, good. Then all we need is the right bait. Something big enough to act as a vector for the pesticide."

Her eyes dart around, and then she points at a nearby tree.

"Look."

I follow her pointing finger and see a series of parallel slashes cut into the tree.

"That is a mark left by a grizzly bear to denote his territory."

"Well, good."

"Good?" I blurt. "How is another predator in the area supposed to be good for us?"

She explained her plan, and I have to admit, it's

rather clever. It will require great risk, but it will be well worth it.

First, I have to track and kill the bear. This isn't too hard, as I find its lair not far from the claw marks on the trees. The bear slumbered inside of a low cave. Only a fool would do battle with a fearsome creature in its own lair, so Paige and I built a fire to smoke it out.

When the bear emerged, I leapt from the cliff overhanging its cave. My axes bite deep, nearly severing its head clean from the great, humped, and furry shoulders. The bear fell to the ground without so much as a groan.

Then comes the grotesque, bloody work. We cut a line down the bear's belly and then scoop out all of its organs and intestines. As I said, bloody work. Paige has worked hard to transform from a weak stomach over the blood, guts, and gaping wounds of our injured tribe into a surprisingly strong stomach. When I question her about it, she laughs.

"Oh, my grandpa taught me how to clean and skin animals when I was younger than Laney is now. This isn't my first eviscerated animal carcass, and it probably won't be the last."

With a lot of effort, we managed to shove the

rusted barrel into the grotesque cavity in the bear's belly. Now comes the hard part, stitching it back together.

"This plan relies upon the tree being somewhat stupid," I say at length as we finish up the stitching.

"Yes, it does, but keep in mind that the tree is magically altered to be a predator. All we're doing is using its predation tactics against it. The irony of herbicide is that it seems like nutrients to the plants it kills. That's how the chemical tricks their roots into drawing it up in the first place."

"Really?"

"That's what my grandpa said. We used natural herbicide on our tiny farm, that and a lot of time bent over in the sun weeding."

I smile, glad to have such a resourceful human on my side. Again, my heart aches for her, but I remind myself this is not the time or the place.

But once the tree is dealt with, I swear I will speak to her about what is between us. Are we still only faking at being mates, or is there something real here? She seemed to reject the idea at first ...

But then she did come looking for me, didn't she? That gives me a renewed sense of hope. That and her clever plan.

The next phase is the most dangerous. I haul

the bear carcass up onto my shoulders ... it is even heavier with the barrel of liquid within it ... and I carry it up the hill to the tree's grove. Perhaps the tree is sated with so many bodies to feed on, or perhaps it hibernates after a fashion. All I know is I am left unbothered as I approach the grove.

I decided against getting any closer. Straining my muscles, I lifted the bear carcass overhead and then hurled it with all of my might. The bear flew a dozen feet and then slammed down on the hard ground ten feet from the tree trunk. I look up at the vine-mummified members of my tribe and shudder. I hope this works for their sake.

At first, nothing happens. I begin to curse under my breath. Then, a vine snakes out from the tree and wraps around the bear. Slowly, the vine winds the bear up toward the trunk. I smile with glee at the sight of vines penetrating the bear's body.

The reddish vines change their hue, taking on a sickly green appearance. The line of green travels all the way up the vine until it reaches the trunk.

"Now what?" I ask her.

"Now, we wait and pray that this works."

For several hours, nothing seems to happen, and I begin to think we may have to try building a fire after all, though that might burn down the entire forest if it gets out of control.

Then, one of the orcs falls from the tree and lands in a groaning heap. I take a step forward, then hold myself in check just in case this is just another trick by the tree.

Then, another of my kin fell, and then the deer and several other animals I had not been able to see higher in the branches. Even if the tree is not dead, it is at the least weakened.

I finally take the risk and move in, rolling my tracker over onto his back. He seems to be asleep, but at least he lives.

"I think your plan has worked," I tell Paige.

"Great," she says. "Only I didn't plan for this next part. How are the two of us supposed to carry almost a score of orcs back to Shattered Rock?"

In response, I took her in my arms and kissed her hard and deep.

17

PAIGE

I stayed with the unconscious victims of the sorcerous tree while Jovak ran out in search of another orc search party. Even if they do wake up, which seems unlikely, most of the victims won't be able to walk without attention from the shamans.

I'm mildly worried that some predator will happen along, and I'll have to defend the victims, but Jovak isn't gone for long. I sighed with relief when I saw him coming down the hill, leading Rolar and his band of warriors.

Then it's time to work as I help build litters out of the scraps we find at the old farmstead. I help bear one of the litters from the back end, which isn't as hard as it sounds considering the emaciated state of the victims.

There's a bit of discussion on the way back as to whether or not the threat presented by the tree is at an end or not. It's possible that the Roundup didn't kill the tree but only weakened it. In any event, we can just avoid that grove from now on, if nothing else.

Jovak sent a runner on ahead of our procession of litters to tell the Shattered Rock tribe to prepare for an influx of new patients. I'm expecting Otunga and her shamans to greet us at the gates.

What I'm not expecting is the huge crowd of onlookers, mostly orcs but some humans too. They give a loud, raucous cheer when we come into view at the bend in the road.

When we pass through the gates, Jovak is all business talking to Otunga, ignoring the orcs chanting his name. I think they're about to build him a statue. What a contrast to the greeting he received when he brought me here … how long ago? It feels like forever, but I think it's only been a week.

I parted ways with the procession so I could go to the school and let Laney know I had made it back safely. To my surprise, she meets me on the way to the schoolhouse.

"Paige!"

Laney ran to me and hugged me tightly. I put my hand on her back and hold her, but I'm a little bit annoyed with her right now.

"Laney, did you sneak away from your teachers to find me?"

She looked up at me with a mix of guilt and stubborn pride.

"Yeah, but I'm not like the other kids. I was practically born on the run. What am I going to learn in the school that I don't already know?"

"Lots of things," I say with a sigh. "Let's get you back before they freak out too much … and you're going to apologize to them, Laney."

"Oh poo," she said, sticking her tongue out.

I dropped her off at school and then checked on Jovak at the temple. The new patients are being cared for as best the shamans are able. Otunga is worried that some of them won't make it even with the best of care, but at least their last days won't be spent suffering at the hands … er, vines, of the tree.

Eventually, Jovak returned home with me, and we made love by the fireplace before Laney returned from school. What follows is a strange dance of denial between the two of us.

For the next few weeks, life returned to what passed for normal. Laney and I live with Jovak, we take our meals with him, and I sleep in his bed every night. We might as well be real mates except for the fact that we both know we're not.

I can tell that it's driving Jovak crazy. I want to say something, but I'm still scared. Maybe I'm afraid if I give voice to what I'm feeling, to what we're feeling, it will become real, and I'll have to deal with it. Or maybe I'm afraid my feelings aren't as strong as they should be. Certainly, Jovak has done everything possible to earn my love, and maybe he even deserves it.

I guess I'm waiting for him to say something or do something. Maybe I want him to claim me for real. All I know is if we don't get this figured out soon, we're both going to go insane.

One morning, I woke and ran right to the privy, where I vomited my guts out. I figured I had eaten something bad or maybe picked up a germ from the schoolhouse.

But I throw up the next morning. And the next, and the next. One night, I tried to stay up until dawn to see if that would keep me from being sick.

Nope, it does not. I still end up sick to my stomach.

Trying not to eat and leaving my stomach empty only gives me the dry heaves, which is somehow worse than actually vomiting. The sickness on schedule every morning in conjunction with certain biological functions being off schedule convinces me of the truth, but I'm terrified to tell Jovak about that too.

One morning, he comes into the privy and puts his hands on his hips.

"Paige, enough is enough. I'm taking you to the shamans."

"No," I say weakly, trying to fend him off. "They have their hands full with real patients right now."

"The tree's victims grow stronger every day, those that survived. You are equally important and deserve to be well. Come."

"Wait, Jovak," I say with a sigh. "I don't need to go to the shamans because I'm not sick."

He cocks an eyebrow at me. "You seem sick."

"I'm not sick, Jovak. I'm throwing up every morning because I have morning sickness."

"Of course, you're sick every morning. That's why I want to take you to the shamans!"

I roll my eyes and groan.

"Damn it, Jovak, why does everything with you have to feel like going around in circles?"

Jovak seized my arms and pulled me in close to him. I can feel his heart beating like thunder. His eyes are swimming with deep meaning, limitless pools roiling with passion.

"How's this for being direct? I love you, Paige. I wish for us to end this charade of being false mates and be real mates instead."

My mouth gaped open, and my heart stopped beating for a moment. When it starts up again, it's with one monstrous thud followed by a rapid staccato that leaves me feeling breathless and dizzy. He loves me. I should tell him how I feel.

Instead, what comes out of my mouth is as unplanned as it is inappropriate, given the circumstances.

"I'm pregnant, Jovak."

His mouth falls open, and his head shakes from side to side.

"But that cannot be."

"Oh, I rather think it can," I scoff. "We've been going at it like rabbits since we started this whole fake mate thing. Which, now that I think about it, has been totally unfair to you. You obviously developed real feelings for me a long time ago."

"I developed real feelings, yes," he says. "And so have you."

I open my mouth to deny it, but nothing comes out. Because I don't want to lie to him, just like before.

But when we had this conversation before, I didn't respond because I honestly didn't know how I felt. Now, though, I can't deny what he's saying because that would be a lie.

My silence is as telling as anything.

"Jovak," I say softly, "what is it that you want from me? I live with you, I tell you everything, I risked my life to come and find you when you disappeared, I sleep with you ...."

I shake my head as tears well up in my eyes.

"What else is that? What else can you call it but love?"

He put his hand on my cheek, and my eyes closed on reflex. I so love the way it feels when he touches me. Why is it so hard to admit that out loud?

"If that's true, then why can't you say it?"

"Because once I say it out loud, then it becomes real, Jovak. It becomes real, and I have to deal with everything that means."

"Like what?" he demands.

"Like the fact that if you have something, it can be taken away from you."

There, I said it. The words came out of my mouth, and the fear shivered through me like a chill wind.

"I don't want to lose you, Jovak, the way I lost my grandpa and everything else I ever cared about except for Laney. And then it looked like I was going to lose her too, and my life, and then you showed up. Like a knight in a shining, uh, loincloth, and ever since then, you've been almost too good to be true, and I guess I don't trust that."

I'm rambling on like crazy. The tears are flowing, but not in racking sobs. Just silent tears were drifting down my face, punctuated by the occasional sniffle.

"So you want me to say it out loud, so the universe can take notice and then take you away from me? I'm not falling into that trap."

"Paige, my love." He took my hand in both of his and squeezed warmly. I so want to let him comfort me, but part of me refuses to budge. I keep my inner self taut as a bowstring. "Don't you see? The real trap is thinking that way. That everything you have might be taken at any time. How can you ever experience real joy with that hanging over you like a dark cloud?"

"Well, now I'm pregnant, Jovak. How does all of that fit into it?"

"Why didn't you tell me when you first suspected?"

"I don't know, I thought maybe … I guess I thought you would believe I was trying to manipulate you, somehow."

"By getting pregnant? That makes no sense."

"You should tell that to human men. They don't seem to understand that part." I sighed and squeezed his hand back. "Jovak, do you really think this is the only way to escape these shackles around my mind and heart? Just like that?"

"I think it will not hurt."

"Okay, fine." I take a deep breath and look into Jovak's eyes. I see all of the things he's done for me, as well as what I've done for him. I see all of the times we had wonderful conversations around the fire or while on the road. I see him teaching Laney how to use a slingshot to down pheasants to add to the stew pot. I see all of the times we made love …

The warmth that blossoms in my heart when I think of these things, if that's not love, then what else is it?

"I love you, Jovak."

The words don't hurt when they come out. Quite the opposite. And I don't feel weighed down with doom. If anything, I feel light and free.

"I love you, Jovak," I say again. "And I'd like nothing more than to be your mate for real this time."

He smiled and moved in for a kiss. I lifted my chin to accept it.

"Well, it's about damn time."

We both turned to see Laney standing there, looking at us.

"How long have you been there?"

"Long enough," she says with a wink. "So, do I get to be a flower girl? Or don't they have those at orc weddings?"

Jovak looks at her and scowls in confusion.

"What is a wedding?"

18
JOVAK

I paced across the floor of Amy and Moldar's hut, grumbling constantly.

"It is ridiculous that I am not allowed to see my mate on the day of this human wedding ritual."

Amy and Laney exchange smirks and then look at me. "You can see her, just not until it's time for the march of the bride."

"March of the bride? Is she going into battle?"

Amy cackles with laughter. "In a manner of speaking, yes, yes, she is. Marriage could be seen as one long battle from a certain point of view."

"Indeed, my mate has the right of things, Chief Jovak." Moldar is leaning heavily on his walking stick, but otherwise, he's looking healthier all the time. Last week, he needed two walking sticks braced under his armpits to get around. Now, he's able to move for short periods of time without any assistance at all.

Most of the tree's victims have recovered, meaning there will be a large turnout for the wedding. Orc mating ceremonies take place under the full moon. Since this was not incongruous with human ceremonies, that has been left intact. There are also many ways in which our two peoples have similar traditions.

For example, it is quite normal for both of our kinds to have a holy person officiate the ceremony. I'm glad about this because it means that humans view mating as sacred like we orcs do.

There are other rituals we share. Both humans and orcs tend to have large feasts after the wedding ceremony. We both have dancing but in wildly different interpretations of the word. We plan to do both kinds of dance after our ceremony.

I look down at my ceremonial garb. The chest plate has been constructed of the armored back of a great lizard the humans call an *alligator*. A fearsome predator whose skin makes for good defense.

It will symbolize the way I aim to protect my mate from all harm after the ritual.

Hanging from each of my biceps are golden bands with feathered charms attached via small silver ingots. The feathers are each from a bird native to these lands, but the tradition goes back to Protheka. A pattern of red, black, and white goes around both armbands, the feathers swaying in the wind coming in through the open window.

Our wedding night is taking place on a rather hot and humid evening. Thank goodness for the breeze which sweeps up the stale air and carries it toward the mountains.

Besides the chest plate and the armbands, I also possess a belt decorated with numerous colored glass beads. The beads tell the story of my exploits as a warrior. When I was a young orc, and my blood was full of fire, long before I ascended to the chieftainship, I added many beads to it. As I grew older, there seemed less time for dangerous accolades. If being chief were easy, I would not have felt the need to go on my long walks and earn the nickname the Longstrider.

"Otunga will be here any moment to anoint you for the ceremony," Amy says. "Are you excited?"

"Of course, he's excited," Laney says with a snicker. "Paige has made him sleep in the living room for the past week so that they'll, um, have plenty of passion, as she puts it."

I stare hard at Laney.

"You are too young to speak of such matters."

"And you are too honest to deny what I just said," she replied with her eyes shining and full of mischief. I sometimes swear that she is worse than her sister. "Remember, I have the power to make Paige call this off."

My body tensed, and my hand slapped over my non-beating heart. Laney giggled. "Don't worry, big brother, you are a perfect match to make our duo a trio."

A rap at the door gives us a start. It was not made by a closed fist as a human would knock or a flat palm, as an orc normally would. It sounded like wood on wood. Therefore, it's probably Otunga rapping on the door with her gnarled staff.

Amy rushed to answer the door while Moldar tried to draw himself up to his full height. He made like he was going to put his crutch to rest in the corner, and I growled at him.

"Do not let pride cause you to take a fall, quite literally in this case, old friend. Keep your crutch.

Otunga will not mind." I chuckled low in my throat. "In fact, she would likely grow quite angry with you for not using the crutch she prescribed as part of your continuing treatment and recovery."

"You are too right about that, my Chief," he replied, keeping the crutch. He still perked up a little when the door opened, and Otunga came in.

"Welcome, Shaman," I say with all due respect.

"Bah," she said with her usual disrespect. "The hour has grown late, and these old bones are tired. Let's get this over with so us sensible orcs can go to bed."

She came fully into the home, followed by several apprentice shamans. The apprentices hold clay pots about the size of my fist. I presented myself to Otunga, who dipped her first two fingers in one pot, smearing them with red pigment.

"These lines represent the blood spilled in battle against the enemies of the Shattered Rock tribe."

She makes two lines on each of my cheeks. Her fingers feel steady despite her advanced age. I think she puts a little bit of her fading magic into the ritual because my skin tingles like I've stood too close to lightning.

"Uncover your heart, Chief Jovak."

I'm not going to argue with the shaman. I take the alligator cuirass off, and she makes a circle around my heart with more red paint. Then she draws a smaller circle inside of it.

"This represents two hearts beating in unison. Two lives conjoined to create a third, a fourth, and, ancestors willing, beyond."

She chants something under her breath as she finishes the ritual. I swear I feel a tingle in my loins, but it could just be that I'm very excited to see my mate, especially after not having lain with her in so very long. I never thought a week could seem an eternity, but it seems I was sadly mistaken.

"My work is done here," Otunga says simply, trying to leave. "Now I must make the long walk to the parade grounds on legs that already ache."

"I could arrange for a litter and have you carried," I offer.

The withering look she gives me makes me want to shrivel up like a grape in the sun until there's nothing left. She takes her leave, and I make no further offers.

"Don't take it personally, my Chief," Amy says. "You know that Otunga likes to complain. You can't take away her one great pleasure."

I have to laugh at that. The sounds of drums echo inside of my breast. It's nearly time.

"All right," Laney says, scooting off the kitchen table where she'd been sitting. Why the child seeks to sit everywhere but on an actual piece of furniture designed for it is beyond me. "I've got to get going if I'm going to do my duty as flower girl and maid of honor."

She says it with such prestige as if it's a sacred duty more important than even the mating between her sister and me. I will not argue.

Laney takes her leave, and I don the alligator vest. Then I realized it would cover the paint on my chest. I don't want to make Otunga angry. Or should I say, angrier?

I headed out down the lane toward the parade grounds. They lurk beneath the Shattered Rock, a cliff that forms a natural defensive barrier for our settlement. The shamans say the shattered rock was hurled up from the earth during a volcanic eruption long ago before we even came to these lands. Sacred or magical, I don't know, but I've grown up in its comforting presence.

The full moon was almost directly overhead when I arrived at the parade grounds. Otunga stands in front of the Shattered Rock, bathed in the glow of luminous silver from the moon. Most of the tribe is there, chanting and drumming, and asking our ancestors to bless the mating between myself and Laney.

I take my place beside Otunga. She nodded and even sort of smiled at me. It seems I have lost a bet with Rolar since her face did not shatter from the effort of doing so.

Then the drums take up a different cadence, a song from the human world. I'm not even able to pay any attention to the sound because my own heartbeat is too loud in my ears. I'm straining my eyes, looking to find the woman I love more than life itself. The woman who will now be my mate for real, instead of just as a convenient ruse.

The woman who is carrying my child. She has not shown any outward signs of it, but soon she will. Soon the tribe will know her stomach is getting larger by one. No more strife over succession.

But the truth is all I really want is to hold her in my arms again and make sweet, passionate love to her all night long.

Then I see her, a ghostly vision all in white. Her hair flows behind her, stirred by the night breeze in a silken sheen. My breath catches in my throat at how beautiful, how radiant she seems. Her smiling face makes me feel light as a feather.

The white garment she is wearing clings to her body as the wind blows it back. Her face is veiled by a thin, translucent, hazy material that doesn't diminish the luster of her full red lips or shining blue eyes. In fact, it enhances them.

Laney is walking in front of her carrying a basket of flowers. She's supposed to be throwing them into the air, but I notice that she's deliberately pelting some of her friends from school with the petals. Well, I suppose Laney is going to be who she is, no matter the circumstance.

I take Paige's hands in my own as we stand in front of Otunga.

"For as many years as the orcs have trod this land and many others, the union of two hearts, two souls, has remained our most sacred of ceremonies. Let this union be bound as tightly as the corded muscles in our chief's arms. Let their children be as wise as their mother, Paige Holdfast, whose courage is legend."

Otunga lifted her hands into the air.

"Under this moon, I declare these two worthy of each other's love. Now, look into each other's eyes, and speak to us all … do you recognize your one true mate?"

Paige and I smile at each other and speak in unison.

"*Yes.*"

19

PAIGE

"Yes."

The word echoes in our hearts and minds as well in the ears of the onlookers at our wedding. Jovak squeezed my hands as the gathered tribe gave a great, jubilant shout. The drums start up like mad, matching the rapid beat of my heart.

"Well, we are now officially wed in the human tradition," Jovak says, his green face stretched with the happiest smile I have ever seen.

"Not quite," Laney says from nearby. "You haven't kissed the bride yet. Duh."

"She's right, you know," I reply with a wink.

"What a terrible oversight on my part," Jovak says with mock severity.

"I know, right? So get over here and kiss me already."

He grinned and then leaned in and took my lips in the most loving, tender way. Of course, then my body reminded me it's been seven long days since it's reared beneath his naked form, and I clasped myself to him. The kiss goes from tender and sweet to torrid in no time flat.

"Save it for after the party," Laney says. "Sheesh, somebody dump a bucket of cold water on these two."

I laugh, though Jovak grumbles. We take our place at the seat of honor, a pile of stones covered with thick animal pelts for our comfort. Young orcs bring us food and drink while the drums reach a new level of intensity.

The male members of the orc tribe take center stage on the parade grounds while the onlookers stretch themselves out into a wide circle to accommodate them. The dance is meant to show off their strength and agility. At times, the orcs stand in lines with military precision, clapping and stomping and chanting in unison. At other times, they whoop, holler, and leap around the parade grounds chaotically.

Once the men have had their turn, the women come out and do a sort of spinning dance, holding totems in their hands. I notice that the younger orc and human females seem to be wearing rather suggestive clothing. Many of them even go topless. I see why in a moment when the men return to the dance floor, pairing up with the women.

Their dance turns seductive and sensual, their bodies pressed together in a swirling, molten sea of fiery embraces. I drink from my glass, but it does nothing to cool me off. I turn and meet Jovak's gaze and see that it's burning just as hot as my own.

"How long do we have to ..." I begin.

"We can leave at any time," he said, sliding off the pile of stones. He held his arms out and helped me down. Then he took my hand and led me off along a well-worn path.

"Where are we going?" I asked as we passed by the trail that leads to his hut. "We're going up. What about Laney? Will she know where we went and that we will be home?"

"Laney will be well taken care of by one of her friends for the night."

"Oh, okay. What's up there?"

"Something special."

I gave him a look, but all he does is wink and pull harder on my hand. I followed him up the path. The sounds of revelry fade behind us, though they never quite vanish. We followed a winding trail that went back and forth on itself as it made its way up to the top of the rock.

At last, I stood on top of the shattered rock, and my breath caught in my throat. It's a lovely view, magnificent and breathtaking. The mountains off in the distance shimmer with reflected moonlight on their snowy caps. Below us, the wedding ceremony is in full swing even though the bride and groom have departed. There is still music and dancing, and with so many flames, the parade ground is nearly as bright as day.

I'm so taken in by the view that I failed to notice there's more up here than just bare rock. I glanced at Jovak to see if this natural splendor took his breath away as much as mine and noticed something behind him.

"What's that?"

I move to a small dwelling about half the size of his hut. It looks ancient, as old as the rock upon which it rests. The outside of the structure is painted with nude orc figures engaged in fleshly pursuits. My mouth fell open when I realized what this place was.

"Oh, I get it. It's for newlywed orc couples, right?"

"It is for mates after the ceremony," he said gently, coming to stand beside me. His big arms wrap around my waist and hold me tightly. I sigh, relaxing into him, reveling in the feel of his warm body pressed against my own.

"The hut is meant to focus the rays of the full moon and ensure a fruitful first joining," he goes on to say.

I cock an eyebrow at him, turning my head enough to see his face.

"So, this is about fertility?"

He nods.

"Isn't it kind of redundant, considering I'm already pregnant?"

Jovak laughs and kisses the top of my head. "Perhaps, but it will also guarantee us privacy."

"Now, that's an idea I can get behind."

His hands roam all over my body, strong fingers kneading the pliant flesh of my breasts, fingers sweeping over my belly and brushing between my legs.

"This is an idea," I say between pants, "that I can

really, really get behind ..."

He kisses me on the neck, and my words are lost in a deep, resonant moan. I'm glad for the sounds of revelry below because I have a feeling I'm going to be making a whole lot of noise, especially after making us both wait for seven of the longest days of my entire life.

My heart thunders in my chest as his soft mouth exhales passionate breaths across my skin. I reach back and caress his long topknot, my limbs flailing already. I grind my bottom against him, and I'm instantly rewarded with a hard twitch from his cock.

Jovak's lips travel across my neck to my shoulder, then I feel pressure from his teeth. Not hard enough to break the skin, but definitely enough to feel their sharpness. I let out a groan when he slides his fingers between my thighs and teases my pussy through the thin material of my dress.

With a growl, Jovak shoved me forward. I caught myself on the curved, round edge of the hut. My cheek is pressed against a green-skinned, big-boobed stick figure being railed by a truly monstrous orc. It's like seeing my future, except I'm not quite that endowed. Probably no woman is. It's an artistic interpretation, after all.

I gasp as Jovak grabs the hem of my dress and draws it up, exposing my legs, then my bottom. He slaps my ass firmly, making it dance for his pleasure.

"Oh god!" I gasp. "Jovak, touch me, please."

"Like this?" he purrs.

His fingers expertly rub through the groove between my pussy lips. I sucked in a deep breath and let it out as an undulating moan. It feels so good. Little flashes of lightning shoot from his fingers into my body, passing through every nerve on their way to my brain. I squeezed my eyes shut, but I still felt the painted artwork by the smoothness of its surface compared to the surrounding stone.

I thrust my bottom out wantonly. My body is ruled by my desires. Jovak continues to pet my pussy while he moves his body closer. His breath is on the back of my neck, then my ear.

"Do you like that, my love?" His velvet whisper sets me off like a freight train, stampeding toward an inexorable climax. It's been so long that I might just explode ... if he ever lets me get there.

"Yes," I gasp as he worms his fingers inside me. It feels so good. I almost can't stand it. I love having him inside me, but what I really want is his cock. I reach behind me and grasp at his loincloth, trying to raise it to get at the prize underneath.

"Is this what you're looking for?" He pulls up his cloth, and I wrap my fingers around his meaty shaft. It positively trembles in my hand, hard as a rod of iron yet flexible like a whip.

He pulls his fingers out of me, but the momentary disappointment doesn't last long. Next, I feel the head of his bulbous member brushing through the slick, wet, open mess of my pussy.

"Oh god, Jovak!" I cry. "Stop teasing. Just put it in me."

"Like this?"

He pushes the head of his cock between my pussy lips, gliding inside inch by inch. I arch my back to accommodate his length while gasping at his girth. He fills me until his balls gently slap against my clit. My guttural groan encourages him to start thrusting.

My eyes flutter closed as he glides into my body with bestial, urgent thrusts. His hand knots in my hair as he presses my cheek against the stone walls of the hut. My moans and cries echo at me from off the wall right beside my lips.

He pounds into me with greater alacrity, one hand gripping my hip, the other my hair. I grind myself into him, moving my body in concert with his. Jovak's animalistic grunts and growls of pleasure turn me on even more.

"Paige, my love," he cries, his voice growing shrill as he strains to hold himself back. He doesn't like to come inside me until I've had at least one orgasm. As long as he keeps going like this, I'm going to have one. He certainly doesn't need to worry about that.

The slapping of our bodies mingles with the drumbeats from below. On instinct, he takes up the rhythm of the drums with his thrusts. It all becomes a cacophony of maddening pleasure so intense that my body trembles.

I feel myself racing for the precipice of the most monstrous orgasms of my life. I draw in a deep breath of air, hold it for a second, and then let it out as pulse after pulse of delight thunders through my body.

Then he comes, and I climax even harder. His cock vibrates and shakes like mad inside me as he empties. Which, of course, sets me off again. I let out cry after cry, barely able to hang on to reality.

Golden fireworks explode behind my eyelids as I ride the waves of pleasure. My fingers scrabble for purchase on the hard stone of the hut, and then he's holding me in his arms, kissing me softly and repeatedly telling me he loves me.

What a wedding night … and we haven't even made it into the hut yet.

Paige and I lay in each other's arms while I stare up through the open canopy of the hut on top of Shattered Rock. Her cheek rests on the side of my chest, her breathing soft and shallow with the rhythms of sleep. Her body is draped over my own, laying on her side while I am on my back. My arm is around her shoulder, fingers loosely splayed over the deltoid while the sounds of revelry continue from below.

The moonlight pours in through the open roof. I stare up at the pockmarked surface and marvel at its beauty. It is nowhere near as beautiful as my mate, the loving woman laying by my side, but it still takes my breath away.

She stirs, and her breathing changes. I know she's awake, but her eyes do not open.

"If this is a dream," she says, her voice thick with recent slumber. "Don't ever wake me."

"I, too, feel as if this is all too good to be true. I keep expecting to wake up and find it's all been a dream or a vision."

It's true. I've never felt so content in all of my life. I used to believe I couldn't stand to spend all of my time at Shattered Rock, that I had to wander or I would lose my mind. Now I have a fixed point to rotate around like the North Star. My life will revolve around Paige from now on, and there's nothing wrong with that.

"Well, I'm pretty sure this isn't a dream," she says, looking up through the open canopy. "I mean, I would never dream of staying in a house with no roof. What happens if it rains?"

"We get wet."

She sits up, breasts swaying with the motion, and grabs a head cushion. Then she strikes me in the face with the cushion playfully.

"Seriously, why doesn't this place have a roof?"

"In order to allow the moonlight inside, to aid in procreation."

"Of course, of course. Is everything about fertility with your people?"

I laughed softly. "No, not everything. Though with how low orcish birth rates are and the rarity of female births in general, it's not surprising that we are rather preoccupied with it. The damnable dark elves defeated us on Protheka in part because they were able to outbreed us."

She shudders in my arms.

"If I never see another dark elf again, it will be too soon."

I clear my throat uncomfortably. She cocks an eyebrow at me. Her naked skin is lovely in the silvery moonlight.

"What is it?"

"My paternal grandfather was a dark elf."

Her eyes widen. "Shut up."

I scowl at her.

"Why do you wish me to stop talking?"

She laughs softly and leans her head back on my chest. "It's a human expression. It means, uh, that it's almost unbelievable, but we know it's true. How did you end up with a dark elf grandpa anyway?"

I take a deep breath and then let it out as a sigh.

It's not a tale I like telling because it means admitting my shame out loud.

"Many years ago, before our people came through the portals, the dark elves and what would eventually become the Shattered Rock tribe had a terrible war. A war that the orcs got the upper hand in. When we finally settled matters, and there was peace, we asked the dark elves if they wanted their prisoners of war back."

My jaw sets hard.

"They refused. They said that any dark elf captured in battle is no longer a dark elf but only so much fecal matter. All of the dark elf prisoners committed suicide by leaping off a cliff after we freed them. All save for one, who was too badly injured to move. That dark elf was named Gronkz, and he was my grandfather. He took an orc wife, an orc name, and tried to live like an orc. Though the legends say he was never truly accepted during his life, he was allowed full orc warrior honors upon his death."

"Wow, that's heavy," Paige says with a sigh. "You poor thing. Is that what Rolar was hinting at when we first met? That you couldn't be trusted because you had dark elf blood?"

"Indeed, though the tribal prejudice has lessened somewhat with time. From what I understand, my father had a much harder time of it. He was dead before I was born."

"My parents died after Laney was born. I still had my gramps, though." She lifted her head from my chest and caressed my cheek. "But surely there are happier things we could be talking about. And even happier things that we could be doing …."

Her hand busies itself with my cock. The once-flaccid member twitches hard and then begins to engorge with blood. She meets my gaze with a sultry look and then lowers her head. Her tongue darts out and licks the end of my prick. My eyes widen, and a gasp forces its way out of my mouth.

"Look how quickly he wakes up," she said, speaking of my cock. Paige's blue eyes are filled with heat as she looks up at me, her mouth full of my rod. I can feel her tongue playing on the underside, and it makes my eyes water.

She suckles, and my hand instinctively goes to the back of her head. Paige pumps her head up and down on me, and the sublime pleasure makes my toes curl to the point of cramping. I release inside of her with a gasping groan, and she doesn't stop. She keeps going, not wasting a drop of my seed.

Paige lifted her head and grinned at me. Turnabout is fair play, so the humans say. I grab her arms and roll her over onto her back. She squeals with delight as I kiss her neck.

I work my way down to her breasts, my tongue darting out to tease her pink nipple. She cries out as I stiffen it with sensuous licks. Then I wrap my lips around it and suckle like there's no tomorrow. I draw my head back, making her breast stretch until it finally pops free. It flops back into place on her chest, assuming its original shape.

I repeat the process several times with each breast before kissing my way down to her belly. She giggles, her hands toying with my topknot. I press her thighs apart and stare at her pussy. The curly, sandy brown hair can't conceal her swollen lips or the way they part to show me the pinkness between them. I dart my tongue through the middle, lapping up her delectable juices and guzzling them down my throat.

"Your pussy tastes so good, Paige," I mumble into the soft folds of her flesh. She cries out, her fingers digging into my scalp. I take her folds in my mouth and suckle on them, getting those precious droplets of her juice into my mouth.

I stretch out her pussy lips like I stretched her breast earlier. Every time I do so, Paige cries out a little louder than before. Her hands are on my topknot, struggling to push my face into a position where I can suck on her clitoris, but I want to tease her some more.

It's only fair, given that she relentlessly teased me during the seven days that she made me wait before our wedding. I well remember her bending over in front of me wearing only the flimsiest of garments or *accidentally* brushing her ass against my cock when she moved past me in our home.

Now it's my turn to make her simmer and suffer ... with the ultimate goal of making her feel the most pleasure imaginable. I let go of her folds and move my tongue in slow circles around her clitoral mound. The pink organ trembles, shaking as if to beg for my attention. I blow across it softly, and it quivers all the more. A deep, desperate moan escapes my love's lips.

"Oh god, Jovak!" she cries. "Please ..."

"Please, what?"

"You're so mean," she gasps. "Please lick my clit ... I sucked you off. Didn't I do a good job?"

"Yes," I said, gently pinching her clit between my fingers. Her body rears up, and she groans so loud it rivals the beating of my heart.

"Then don't I ... deserve ... this?"

"Yes," I say, and then I latch onto her clitoris and suckle as if my life depends upon it. She sucks in a ragged gasp of air, then hisses long and loud. She repeats this several times, and then her nails dig into my scalp with renewed urgency.

"Oh god! I'm gonna come!" Her scream splits the air, and then she deluges my face with a torrent of her pussy juice. I keep suckling and licking until her body stops thrashing like a fish pulled from a stream.

At last, she flopped back onto the bed, her chest rising and falling with heavy pants. Her half-lidded eyes look up at me, and a happy grin forces its way to her face.

"You're so good at what you do," she gasps. "I'm a lucky woman."

"No," I say, shaking my head. "I am the lucky one here, Paige. The luckiest day of my life was when I found you."

"Yeah, mine too." She laughs softly and plays with my hair as I rest my chin on her belly. "I mean, at first, it was one of the worst luck days I'd ever had, but then you happened along and got to be my big hero in shining … um, well, my hero in a loincloth. Since I stopped acting in fear, I have a handsome mate, my sister is safe and has friends, and you have given Laney and me a huge family." She rubs her flat stomach and says, "A huge family that is about to grow by one."

I laugh and shrug. "I will put on shining armor if it will please you, my love. I would do anything to make you happy."

"Oh god, I believe that."

She hugs me tightly, wrapping her arms around my head. I nestle my face into her soft bosom and sigh.

Then, I push her onto her back again and rear up on my knees. I wrap my fingers around my cock and smile at her.

"Oh, it's so big," she says with mock terror. "What are you going to do with that, you big, bad orc?"

"I'm going to stuff your pussy with it."

"Oh no," she says sarcastically. "Please, anything but … oooh."

I glide into her, my cock sliding in and stretching her pink walls. She grips me as tight as a vise, her pussy convulsing as if she seeks to draw me in even farther.

I rock my hips and thrust into her. Her mouth forms an O, and then she throws her head back and moans deeply, desperately. Her legs wrap around my waist, ankles crossing just above my buttocks. Then she gives as good as she gets. Our bodies move in sync, seeking that perfect connection that so many seek but never find.

Our passionate cries echo up to the moon, who thankfully has seen so much, she doesn't turn red with embarrassment.

21

PAIGE

The late afternoon sun dapples shadows through the trees over the meadow as I settle onto a smooth boulder near a merrily babbling stream. Gronk stirs a bit from his slumber, but his eyes remain shut. He instantly roots around, looking for a nipple.

"Such a hungry boy," I say with a chuckle, fishing my breast out of my dress so he can latch on. Nearby, Laney and Jovak talk about lures.

"No, no," Laney says with a sigh, rolling her eyes to the sky. "Are you kidding me right now? That is so *not* how you tie a fly-fishing line."

"It looks good to me," Jovak says with a frown, staring at his handiwork.

"If you try to use that lure, you're going to be sorry," Laney says.

"I suppose that you can do it better?" he asks.

"Naturally," she says. Then she breaks into a song. "Anything you can do, I can do better. I can do anything better than you …."

Jovak smiles. By this point, well used to this game.

"No, you can't," he says, also singing.

"Yes, I can! Anything you can sing, I can sing better …."

I smile as I feed my son by the stream. The two of them carry on for a bit, and then Jovak unties his lure and allows the master, that being my eleven-year-old sister, to show him how it's supposed to be done.

When I agreed to become Jovak's mate for real … not that I really had much choice, given how deeply I love him … I was a bit worried about what would happen to Laney. Would he insist she move somewhere else, like Amy's, perhaps?

No, he did not. Nothing changed between Jovak and Laney. Except, maybe their bond became stronger. At times, he is like a father to her, providing advice and comfort. At other times, he's like her big brother, gently teasing her while also showing her how to do many tasks.

And at other moments, Laney becomes the teacher and him the student. Like when I was grossly pregnant with Gronk, and Jovak came in the door and cheerfully told me I was swollen up like a full moon. Apparently, this is a compliment from the orc's viewpoint. It didn't go over well with me, naturally.

Laney helped Jovak see his error and overcome the initial hurt feelings he experienced at another perceived rejection. Then he learned from his mistake and came and delivered the most heartfelt apology I'd ever known.

The two of them are wonderful together, and I count my blessings. I have many to count these days.

After our mating, the dark elf army moved closer. Jovak sent out riders to keep an eye on them, but the dark elves didn't attack. They put up their stronghold a good distance away, outside of the lands the Shattered Rock tribe claims. On a clear day, you can see their castle from the top of Shattered Rock. It's a worry for the future, but not for a sunny day like today.

Besides, I've found my happily ever after. The

world might be a cold, cruel, and sometimes terrifying place, but my family is my safe space. My son, my husband, and my little sister. All of us living together, if not in perfect harmony, then a close enough facsimile to count.

Jovak no longer wanders. He is not the Longstrider any longer. His people have changed his nickname.

Now he's Jovak the Kinfinder because he found his lost kin and saved most of them. Most of the victims of the tree have made a full recovery … physically. There seem to be some side effects. Amy tells me that sometimes Moldar wakes in a cold sweat, having dreamt of being with the tree.

When he was stuck with the tree, he shared some of his consciousness with it. It was a two-way street, and Moldar and the other victims believe that the evil that spawned the tree didn't die with the tree itself. They think the evil lives on, and they are somehow connected to it.

But whatever problem comes along, whatever dangers we have to face, I feel no fear. I know that Jovak and I can handle it. Technically, the chief's wife doesn't have any official power, but many of the orcs in the tribe address me as *chieftess* when speaking to me. It's a little embarrassing. What's even more embarrassing is when Jovak tells the story of how he found me.

In reality, I'd been facing a single orc in combat, and by and large, I did more talking than fighting, trying to stall him so Laney could recover and escape. It was a fight where I was badly outmatched. I only got a good hit in because I tricked my opponent.

And to be honest, I wouldn't have gotten that far if he hadn't so terribly underestimated me.

But when Jovak tells the story, I wasn't facing off against one orc, but a dozen and my bravery and skill were such that only their sheer numbers were going to overcome me. Worse, a lot of people think that Jovak is downplaying my skills, if anything, and they see me as some kind of wise Zen sword master, and I'm anything but.

I have been training with Jovak just to help me lose the baby weight. He doesn't care. He says he loves my soft belly, but I care. Besides, as the chieftain's wife, I don't want to look like I'm soft. I have a reputation to uphold, after all.

"There," Laney says, pointing at her handiwork. "Now *that* is how you tie a fly-fishing line."

"It is a good knot indeed," Jovak says. Then he gives her a mischievous look. "Of course, if I had such tiny and spindly fingers, I could probably do much the same."

"Oh, what is it about a craftsman who blames his tools?" Laney snorts. "It's the same thing of an orc who blames his fingers."

"Hey," I call from my rock. Both of them turn to face me. "Not all of us can survive on my breast milk. How about you two stop arguing and start catching our dinner?"

Jovak laughs, and Laney sticks her tongue out at me. Then she turns a grin on Jovak.

"How about a little wager, Jo Jo?"

I do believe Laney is the only one who could possibly get away with calling him that.

"A wager?" he asks, intrigued. "Of what sort?"

"How about we see who can catch the most fish before dinnertime?" Laney asks with a bit of an edge to her voice. "The loser has to wash the dishes for the next week."

"Hmm," he says, "I do hate washing dishes. Very well, I accept your wager."

They shake on it.

"May the best orc win," Jovak says.

"Hey," Laney gasps. "No way. May the best woman win. And in case you don't know, that's me."

Their good-spirited contest carries well into the evening. By the time the first stars wink into existence overhead, it's clear Laney has more fish in her pile than Jovak.

"How are you doing this?" he gasps. "Are you a sorceress singing to the fish in their own language?"

"I don't need magic to beat you," she said, sticking out her tongue and giggling.

"It really wasn't a fair contest, dear." I gently tuck my sleeping son into his blankets and smile up at my mate. "Laney has been fly-fishing since she was old enough to hold a rod and reel. You didn't stand a chance."

"Bah," he said. "She tied my lure wrong on purpose to make me lose."

Laney gasps, and then Jovak laughs.

"I'm jesting. Congratulations on your victory, Laney. But next time we go fishing, I will not be some mere novice."

Laney and I scale and clean the fish while Jovak builds a fire. I notice a few orcs from the tribe standing guard a discreet distance away. They'll allow their chief and his family to range out of the settlement, but at night, we always end up with a few bodyguards.

We lay the fish out to smoke on a lattice of stout sticks and folded leaves. I find some wild thyme and onions and use them to season the meal. I feel the same way I did when we used to do this with my grandpa, only better.

Better because I have a husband and a son to share it with. I know Gramps is looking down on us and smiling.

When there's nothing left of the fish but smiles and greasy fingers, I sit propped up against a rock, my son in my arms and my husband with his arm over my shoulders. His other arm is over Laney's shoulders. My sister snores softly as the moon rises over the meadow.

"I love you, Paige," he said softly, kissing me tenderly.

"I love you, too, Jovak. Thanks for a perfect day."

"Thanks for a perfect life."

ABOUT THE AUTHOR

New York Times and USA Today Bestselling Author

Hi! I'm Milly Taiden. I love to write sexy stories featuring fun, sassy heroines with curves and growly alpha males with fur. My books are a great way to satisfy your craving for paranormal romance with action, humor, suspense and happily ever afters.

I live in Florida with my hubby, our son, and our fur babies: Speedy, Stormy and Teddy. I have a serious addiction to chocolate and cake.

I love to meet new readers, so come sign up for my newsletter and check out my Facebook page. We always have lots of fun stuff going on there.

SIGN UP FOR MILLY'S NEWSLETTER FOR LATEST NEWS!

http://eepurl.com/pt9q1